THE GOSPEL ACCORDING TO CANE

THE GOSPEL ACCORDING TO CANE

BY Courttia Newland

This is a work of fiction. Names, characters, places, and incidents are the product of the author's imagination or are used fictitiously. Any resemblance to actual persons, living or dead, as well as events or locales, is entirely coincidental.

Published by Akashic Books
©2013 Courttia Newland

ISBN-13: 978-1-61775-133-2
Library of Congress Control Number: 2012939271
First printing

Akashic Books
PO Box 1456
New York, NY 10009
info@akashicbooks.com
www.akashicbooks.com

Acknowledgments

As always, much gratitude to the ancestral spirits; I really felt your guidance with this one.

Much love to those earthly ones who kept me on the path: Sharmila, Senenti, Marlene Denny, James Miller, Brian Chikwava, Sherin Nicole. Thanks for being with me.

To the ones who fed my imagination: Alex Mckenzie, Joyce Treasure, Ramona Scotland. Thank you.

To my draft readers: Yvvette Edwards, Linton Kwesi Johnson, Alistair Fruish, Victor LaValle, Carolyn Hart, Ellie Searley, Rosalind Waterman. Much appreciation.

Also, to the amazing authors who influenced this novel: Richard Price, Percival Everett, Annie Proulx, Steven Millhauser, Earl Lovelace, and the late Rosa Guy. Eternal gratitude to you all.

And the ones who made it happen: Johnny, Johanna, and the Akashic team, Ed Wilson, Hellie Ogden, and Chris Abani. Thanks for looking out, brother.

For Mum

We worry about what a child will become tomorrow,
yet we forget that he is someone today.
—Stacia Tauscher

I write, therefore I am.

❧

Some people say pain is relative. They claim an earache, a bumped funny bone, and a broken leg can all be excruciating or no more than a tickle according to the subject's threshold. I happen to disagree, at least beyond a certain point. For me, there is some pain that has the capacity to hurt anyone. An amputation with or without anesthetic, for instance, or a bullet in the chest. Pain of that nature is tangible even though it can't be seen, like the presence of oxygen. Pain that fervent is beyond refute.

❧

I first noticed him in Portobello Market, on a Thursday if I recall. It was one of those balmy afternoons of mid-September we get these days, nothing like summer but warm enough to wear a thin dress and cardie, not worry about a jacket. I was having a nice time actually. I'd spent the day in Holland Park with one of my neighbors, a local old girl called Ida. We'd sat in the café for hours drinking coffee and talking about absolutely nothing. I went for a wander and a read in the Japanese Garden before I took a slow walk, stopping briefly to admire the peacocks and rabbits. I strolled down Notting Hill and made a right turn, which led me into the market. I was walking pretty fast once I got there, trying not to talk with too many people, buying fruit from the organic stalls beneath Portobello Green, nothing substantial, as Abel and Cole had made a delivery. I was browsing really, enjoying the sun on my back. And then I saw him.

He was standing next to the green doors of the office units under the motorway. A tall boy, though it was immediately apparent he was more like a young man than a child. His shoulders were wide beneath his black hoodie, and his face had none of the puppy fat associated with younger children, the ones I was used to teaching, or trying to teach at least. The loose wisps of a beard he'd tried to grow with mild success, cotton candy on his cheeks rather than peach fuzz, told me how much of a man he actually was. For the millionth time I found myself thinking how my own child would have looked after all these years, and then I turned, not wanting to follow the thought to its obvious conclusion.

I ducked my head to examine a solid mango, yellow and green with a red blush. When I chanced a look upward, the young man was boring into my eyes. I'd seen that look before. The young people in the After-School Club would often stare at each other that way, sometimes even me. I tried to tell them it never would have been accepted back home, where our kin had been born, either Africa or the West Indies depending on the child. A look like that would have been slapped from our faces. Maybe that was part of the trouble.

Obviously, I couldn't say anything like that. You can't tell young people what you think of their behavior if you haven't known them since they were toddlers, and even then you keep a close eye on your tongue. Knives and guns are commonplace, and there are even local stories of people being shot for asking the young not to smoke in a public space. So I tried not to get too upset when I saw the tall youth stare, even though I was nervous. I steeled myself and looked him in the eye as if to challenge him physically rather than verbally, to remind him of his mother and make him think twice. When he remained that way, lounged against the wall with his lip curled as if to say he didn't give a damn who saw him, I was struck by the horrid thought that it might be lust, rather than anger, that drove him. All right, he wasn't winking, or giving any signs of a come-on, or being the least bit amorous, but he wasn't acting in a threatening manner, or saying anything, or coming over either. The more I thought about it, the more I ducked my head and looked away before snatching another quick glance, the more that curled lip reminded me of someone trying to smile who didn't quite know how. That scared me even more than if he'd been swearing.

I put down my blushing mango and walked away with my head down, trying to be casual and not stumble. Someone called my name, but I ignored whoever it was and kept going, across one road, down a block, a right turn at the corner off-license which took me away from the market and into a residential area just past the estate. I didn't look back and didn't run. I kept my eyes on the pavement and watched my feet move. I cut through the first estate block, turned right, took a left onto Goldbourne. When I smelled coffee and saw the gathered Moroccan men outside market stalls, the out-of-town shoppers, and kids coming home from school chirping like morning birds, I breathed a sigh of relief. Nothing to worry about. I took a look, just to make sure.

He was there. Leaning against another wall, watching me breathe in the atmosphere. I almost jumped when I noticed, couldn't hide my panic. I began to walk again, faster this time.

I'd been a bit clever, grateful for the brains my late father passed on. My flat was actually one street behind me. Once on Goldbourne, shielded by numerous people enjoying the late-afternoon sun, I sprinted back down the next street, going in a rough square until I was on the mouth of my road, breathing hard. Thank goodness I didn't smoke anymore. I took a quick check to make sure he wasn't behind me, and then forced another sprint out of my weary legs, along the cul-de-sac, jangling keys like a jailer. My hands were shaking. My heart was thudding in my chest.

Just before I entered, I took another look. The street was a barren land. I slammed the door.

❦

Things that keep me going:

- My journal
- Seth
- The After-School Club
- Hope

Damn. That's pitiful.

- Jackie and Frank (?)

Even worse.

❧

A friend of mine, Keith, back when I was in Teacher Training College, came into class one day wincing and holding his jaw. He shuddered through our morning lecture, knocking back aspirins and taking gulps from his plastic cup of water as often as the directions would allow. After class, he told me he had a rotten back tooth, had booked an afternoon appointment at the dentist's. I was amazed he'd even come to class, let alone decided to have his tooth out on the same day. He was hoping to get someone to go with him, as his brother had said he would, but couldn't make it because of a job interview. Before I said yes, he warned that he'd opted to have the extraction done without a shot. Being a black belt in tae kwon do, in training since his teens, Keith said he could conquer pain.

I didn't really want to go. I had hours of study to catch up on, but we were such good friends that Keith already knew my timetable, so he also knew I was free for the rest of that day. When we got there, my hands were shaking and my bangles tinkled like wind chimes. I thought it would be a simple matter of sitting in the waiting room and reading *Best* magazine until Keith came out, woozy and proud. I'd congratulate him and we'd leave, that would be it.

Keith was his usual self, way too friendly, cracking bad jokes with everyone in the waiting room. When they called his name, some dizzy receptionist said they didn't normally allow it, but it would be fine if his girlfriend went through, and the dentist smiled and beckoned, and I tried to protest and tell them I'd stay and read about the woman's sister who slept with her husband while she was sick in hospital with cancer, but it never came out with quite the strength I wanted. Next thing I knew, they were gone.

They made me sit on a little chair in the corner of the tiny room. There were posters of assorted Mr. Men with toothaches and bandaged jaws, and Superman X-raying the lungs of a smoker. The room smelled of chemicals and that pink liquid they make you wash your mouth out with. Keith climbed into the chair and they asked him once again if he was fine to do the extraction without a shot, and he said yes, it was no problem, he'd been trained. The assistant started up the suction gun, put it in Keith's mouth. His hands were practically bone white they were clutching the armrests so hard. I couldn't look, but I couldn't close my ears either.

I won't go into exactly what I heard, but suffice to say there was an awful scrape of metal against enamel that instantly made me want to cry, and of course Keith's screams, which only came about halfway when he couldn't take anymore, and it was too late to go back and give him the dose, so they just had to carry on until he was bellowing like a bull who'd been stuck by the matador, and when I looked down I was horrified to see blood and slivers of Keith's brown tooth peppering the plastic tunic they'd given me. His arms weren't clutching the armrests by then, they were trying against his own will to fight what was happening, to stop the dentist. Once his leg involuntarily lashed out and kicked the assistant, who was dripping sweat, face completely white, and the dentist said Keith was lucky it hadn't been him or else he would have drilled through his cheek or somewhere worse. There was muffled swearing and grunts, sometimes from the dentist, most of the time from Keith. It went on for half an hour or more. I would have left but my legs didn't have any strength to carry me and I knew that if I got up I would faint. Eventually there was a tug from the dentist, a *plink*, and the offending tooth was lying in a kidney-shaped tray, glistening like rotten wood. There was blood too, but I didn't peer into the tray long enough to say what that looked like.

The dentist told Keith they would go ahead with his stitches. That was my cue. I stumbled into the waiting room, where the few people still there stared. The dizzy receptionist couldn't meet my eye. I hoped she blamed herself. I think the dentist must have given Keith the shot this time, because that part of the proceedings was pretty quiet. Not long afterward, Keith came out. He was weak at the knees, a few shades paler than when he'd gone in, and his eyes looked glazed and far away, but he'd done it. He might have overestimated his abilities, but he'd come out on the other side. I admired that.

Years later, my own threshold was tested to its limits in an entirely different manner. I was faced with the challenge of seeing how much I could take before I screamed aloud and embraced the pain, like Keith, or gave up and accepted the shot. I'm not sure which of the above I actually managed, which of those options could be deemed good or bad. I'll leave that for you to judge.

This is my account. This is the journal of my pain.

✺

There is nothing more agonizing than the death of your own child. No hurt that hits harder, no pain that goes deeper, no tears that burn more fiercely than those produced by the terrible knowledge that you have outlived your daughter or son. Being part of a profession focused on the welfare of children, I'd heard this said repeatedly before I endured the loss. There is no verbal platitude or empathy that can soothe the pain of that constant wish, your continual search, for the person you love more than anything else in the world, the person you have lost.

Actually, scratch the above. Or if it can't bear to be scratched, then at least add a footnote†.

✺

I write, though I am not a writer. My concern is not narrative, character, or chronological structure, but the rearing of children in modern society, the ills a lack of proper parenting can produce, and the strange phenomena of pain. What a lot of P's I have in that sentence. Never mind. If I were a writer, I would have known how to extract such lazy alliteration. My point is, if a tale does emerge from these disparate, rambling pages, then so be it, though I have to be fair and let any potential reader know that was never my intention. My vocation

---

† The only thing more agonizing than the death of your child is being uncertain whether your child is alive or dead.

is/was a teacher of secondary school–level English, but I gave that up a long time ago. Now I use my skills in a more direct fashion, with children on the margins, the ones I feel need it most.

I graduated from my father's former polytechnic a Bachelor of Education, just over twenty-two years ago. I was immediately snapped up by a prestigious private school and worked there for almost eighteen months. I had a beautiful house, a husband, a loving family, a newborn son, even a lovely dog. Now, only my limited family remain, for what little good it does. That person, the woman I was, is not exactly gone as much as she has faded into the background, distant like a stationary object viewed from a speeding train. I am neither sad nor concerned to see her go. She is no use to me now.

I took a long look in the mirror before I wrote the following paragraphs, in order to have a better understanding of the woman I am. I think it was a bad idea. I haven't gone as far to actually ban mirrors, but I suppose I do tend to duck my head twice a day as I brush my teeth, and I forgot to check how my clothes fit when I stopped buying new things. What for? My local charity shops are probably the best stocked in the country, with more designer wear than Westfield's. I'm joking, of course, but you get the idea. I've a sneaking suspicion a charity shop off Portobello Road and one on Leeds High Street bear not even the slightest comparison.

So I gave myself the old once-over and I have to admit, it scared me quite a bit. I've worn my hair short for twenty years, but despite that I still had the image of myself as I'd been in college, with that long ponytail halfway down my back. Silly cow. I'd put on quite a bit of weight, not that I was fat, mind you, but the skinny thing with the figure of a wooden clothes peg was long gone. My cheeks were chubby, and my maize complexion looked much paler than I remembered. What scared me were the rings around my eyes. That gave my age away more than anything, and I was reminded of the fact I would be fifty in less than six years, and I couldn't look anymore. I had to go in the bedroom and lie down, tell myself I wouldn't be doing that again.

After ten minutes I rolled off the bed. I opened my laptop and sat at the desk and kept typing.

෨

Books I have recently read:

- *Cannery Row*, John Steinbeck
- *The Water Cure*, Percival Everett
- *The God of Small Things*, Arundhati Roy
- *Love in the Time of Cholera*, Gabriel García Márquez

෨

When my nerves subsided, I made dinner. The light was fading and the random creak of bicycle gears over mute voices lurked outside my window. The kids were out, doing whatever they did when the sun went down. I wished the government could think of some way to stop them loitering, but that didn't seem very likely.

I was sitting on my sofa, contemplating whether I should switch on the TV and be bombarded by some inane late-afternoon program, when my letter box rattled, the bark of metal making me jump. Suddenly the gloom got more acute, the shadows more threatening. It was the tall boy, I knew it. He'd found a way to work past the intercom system and follow me to my flat. The estate kids did it all the time, waiting for someone to come inside, then slipping past the door. Maybe I hadn't been so clever.

The letter box rattled again, impatient. Stopped. I pushed my nose into the sofa, glad I hadn't switched on the TV, waiting to see if he'd go.

Held my breath.

It rattled again, for a long time.

Stopped.

I took a slow peek above the sofa.

Silence. Compressing the room with its weight. Then:

—Hello!

A beam of light from the open letter box, imaginary eyes. I dropped against my sofa cushions.

—I know you're in there!

Shit. Maybe he *had* seen me. But he could be bluffing. It was dark . . .

—C'mon . . .

More rattling, awful, tense silence. I strained to hear better.

—Open the bloody door . . .

Risking another quick peek. Still doubting. It was probably him, but I didn't want to take the chance.

—Beverley, open the bloody door, will you!

It *was* him. He was going to be so annoyed.

I got up from the sofa, sheepish, opened up. Seth came striding into the flat, all six-foot-plus, towering above me. Even though his face was cast in shadow I could feel his frown.

—Why the hell didn't you let me in?

—I didn't know it was you. You should have phoned or something; let me know you were coming.

—I told you. Last week.

—Well, you should have buzzed the intercom. I turned and walked into the flat. That's what it's for.

He waited, slow spinning, a looming figure.

—Why are the lights off?

—Because I felt like it. Is that why you dropped by, to interrogate me? Get some practice in?

—Don't be daft. The lights came on. It galled that he knew exactly where they were. I said I was coming.

I sat on the sofa, deflated, falling straight into the usual act I performed whenever Seth came round. Raised voices could be heard outside, but I couldn't tell what they were saying. I was quite relieved he had come, really. I should say that, seeing as I'm telling the truth. I couldn't help thinking about the tall boy on the street watching the flat, even though I hadn't seen him follow me. It was an irrational fear made real by my imagination; I knew that, but it didn't make me any less scared.

—Can I sit down?

I'd forgotten he was there.

—Yeah, sure.

He took the space next to me, leaving enough room to make me comfortable. We sat in silence for what felt like a long time. I could see his reflection in the dark square of the TV screen, squeezed into his plain suit jacket, body stretched like elastic, everything too long—

his hands, his feet, his torso, his head. Seth's features reminded me of an old shoe that had been walked in for miles, cracked and frayed in places, a bit curled by the weather.

—So . . . How've you been?

—Not bad. Getting by.

—How are the little tykes doing?

—Very well. We've been reading Shakespeare. *Othello*.

—Oh, good. How are they finding it?

—Hate it, actually. We laughed, him cautious, me reluctant. Though it did promote some discussion. About the role of black people in the war . . .

I trailed off. Seth is one of the few people who doesn't mind talking about race. Some people behave like the very mention is a dirty word and don't thank you for reminding them it actually exists. Still, I always feel that slight touch of hesitance whenever I raise the issue in his presence. I suppose I'm never sure when his patience might run out.

—Sounds fascinating. I'd like to drop in . . .

I said nothing, looked at the floor. Seth cleared his throat.

—Oh yes, I forgot. Don't want to harm your reputation. Sorry.

—It's not that. It's just if one of them gets arrested, God forbid, and they're taken to the station, and they see you . . .

—You don't have to explain, I understand. Impartiality is key. I respect what you're doing, I wouldn't undermine that.

—Thanks.

He was drumming his fingers against his knees, irritating me, but I didn't want another argument.

—How's work?

Seth heaved a sigh.

—Not pretty. Same old, same old.

Nervous laugh.

—You're doing a great job. You know that, don't you?

His worn-shoe face gaped surprise.

—You think so?

—Yes. Of course I do.

He was smiling. He leaned back in the sofa, threw over an arm.

—You know, after all these years I thought we might not be your favorite people. I thought you might resent us.

—Oh, I do. I was only talking about you. The rest of the force can go hang as far as I'm concerned.

The smile froze. The arm returned to rest by his side.

—Sorry.

—No, no, that's quite all right. I totally understand.

I wanted him to tell me to fuck myself, punch the sofa, jump up in a rage. I knew it wouldn't happen. Seth was the proverbial gentle giant. I hated being his little pressed flower.

—Would you like a cup of tea?

—Oh, yeah. Thanks, love.

I went into the kitchen and put the kettle on. Puffed a long, silent breath. Made the tea and went back with a mug in each hand.

—There you are.

—Ta, that's great.

He took the mug, put it by his feet. Maneuvered those huge knees toward me.

—Are you okay?

—According to my shrink, no . . .

He didn't laugh.

—Only joking. Course I am.

—You seem a bit upset.

—No more than usual. I mean . . .

—Can I help?

Seth put a hand on my knee. It was bare where my dress had ridden up. Very strategic. The hand was rough and hot.

—Seth . . .

—Don't be like this, Bev. We're good, aren't we?

I hate my name being shortened, but couldn't be bothered to say what he knew. There was a tingle in my belly. I put down my mug of tea. Lay back. Seth got to his feet and pushed my dress further up, placed his head on my lap. His breath was warm against my skin. His hair was black-and-white ashes. I could smell the gel he'd used. I put my hand on his neck, massaged. The tendons were thick, solid. He began to kiss my thighs. I let him.

❦

I suppose you must be wondering why I decided to write this at all, if my prime intention wasn't to convey a character's physical and emotional journey through a linear narrative arc. To tell the truth, something I hope I've managed all through this journal, I wasn't even sure I wanted to write my story at all until I went to the club one day. It was pretty hot in the room. I was running on a short fuse. We were talking about the book we were reading, or I was reading at least; getting the little tykes to look at anything was more and more difficult, what with the Internet and those stupid little phones and the PS-whatever-it-is they're always on about. Anyway, we were discussing the section I'd read from *Shoedog* by George Pelecanos, which I'd probably got them to talk about for more than five minutes because it was a violent crime novel rather than one concerning human psychology, or world history, or black achievement, all of which most of them hated, when Chris pipes up and says:

—Miss, what do people write for?

And I wasn't really listening as I was about to correct his bad grammar, then what he'd said really hit me. For a minute I was taken aback, firstly because it was a good question, and secondly because I *didn't have the answer*. So I thought, and the kids all looked, and I opened my mouth and out came:

—People write because they've got an urge to express themselves. Because they have something they want to say that they feel compelled to share with the world. Because they've seen something they can't comprehend and they're trying to work it out through the act of writing. They write because they want to make sense of their pain.

Like I said, I'm not an author and I hope whoever finds this isn't, as I'm probably talking complete faff. The thing is, it didn't matter; the kids lapped it up. It was one of those fine moments when we connected and even though I'd finished speaking they were staring as if they wanted more, and I was standing there twirling the novel in my hands because I couldn't think of anything else. Then Jeff said:

—Yeah, like Tupac when he wrote "Dear Mama." He had an urge to express how it felt to ave a crack ho fuh a mum, an sell drugs an ave p's in is pocket so he could take care ah her, innit, an he wanted to share is pain wid mans like us . . .

And that was it, they were off on another topic from which it took five minutes to bring them back, mainly due to my staring off into space, thinking about what I'd said and how it might be good to do something like that, write down everything, all my thoughts and feelings, and see where it led, knowing it couldn't possibly be anything but good for me, and might even make sense of the past twenty years' quiet madness.

So here it is. The whole sordid tale. Enjoy.

∽

Seth left straight afterward. That was the deal and I suppose he's reliable that way. I had a shower and got dressed, nothing special, just tracksuit bottoms and a hoodie. I took my printouts, locked up, and went to the club.

I've been running the After-School Club for years. The kids come and go, of course, but I stay. At first, after my worst nightmare, I was set so far adrift I wasn't even sure I could return. I'd sold a house, lost a husband, lost a child, a life. I would sit in my two-bedroom council flat and drink tea to stave off hunger, sit with the TV on and not watch, wasting away. My sister came by every once in a while, but she had her own problems and mine had been dragging on, and she just didn't have the stamina. If it wasn't for Ida, the old girl from six doors down, it could have been months before I laid eyes on a living soul.

There was no life-changing moment, no epiphany. I think I just had enough. One day I was lying in bed, like I had on all the other days, and I suddenly knew what I could do. It was that instant. I even had the name. I got out of bed, went to my nearest youth center, which happened to be less than two blocks away, and asked if they would be willing to let a certified teacher run free classes in a back room for a couple of evenings a week. I had no immediate need of money. My father had provided well and when my husband and I sold the house, we made a tidy sum. There was no financial reason not to give something back.

On my way to the club, I realized how fast I was walking, made myself slow. The estate windows were like spider's eyes, row after row, and the doorways were dark, open maws.

Hayley and Sam were in the parking lot. They saw me and jumped, chins raised to the darkening sky as though appealing for help. I was watching their hands and so I saw the quick movement, the arcing glow fall into the gutter, the smoldering.

—Evening.

—Evening, miss.

Eyes on black dust, grease-proof fried chicken paper.

—What did I say to you both about smoking?

Hayley shot Sam a look, teeth gritted, caught herself, and turned to me. She was a blank-faced blonde, nice-but-dim parents, nine-to-fivers, normal working-class fare. A good girl, bit of a raver from what little I knew. I guessed she slept with Sam once in a while because

I saw him come out of her house early enough in the mornings on occasion. Wasn't sure how her father felt about that, didn't ask.

—Sorry, miss.

—Sorry, miss.

—It's not me you should say sorry to, it's your lungs. Wait until your thirty, you'll see. Have you brought your homework?

I walked into the club. They followed.

—Yes, miss.

—How did you find it?

—It was good. Hayley was smiling. I enjoyed it.

—Sam?

He wasn't looking, eyes darting from point to point as he entered the youth center. It was focus that was the hardest, especially for the boys. I don't know if that's due to nurture or nature, what they eat or how they live. Sam wasn't bad, or dim, just easily distracted.

—It was all right, miss.

—But you did it, right?

—Yeah, definitely.

—Good.

The room was a small space, but my class wasn't exactly large. As usual, I was pleased to see them all. There were, of course, occasions over the years when kids wouldn't turn up for various reasons. Sometimes not come back. Vanessa was sitting in her normal spot, expectant and quiet, reading. I could always rely on her. Jeff and Chris were sitting on the tables, something they knew I hated, swaggering and talking loud, probably for Vanessa's benefit. They jumped and took their seats. Heshima, who'd been adding a comment here and there, slid into the place next to Hayley. As far as I knew they'd been friends since nursery school.

I stood at the front, waiting for them to find their comfort zones, get settled. They looked quite eager, a good sign.

—Evening, class.

—Evening, Ms. Cottrell . . .

Intoned in unison.

—How's everyone doing tonight?

Scattered *all right*s, noses wrinkled, seat stretches, yawns.

—How are you, miss?

From Jeff, a stocky, short youth. Bad parents, bad friends, always loudest.

—Not the best today, but I'll get by . . .

—Ah, what's wrong, miss?

As soon as I said it I knew I shouldn't have gone there. Hayley's arm was still half-raised, a residue from real school, the remainder of the class staring.

—Oh nothing, just a bit under the weather.

Lots of nods. If there was anything they understood, it was that.

—Okay, so let's get started with today's lesson, shall we? How did you guys do with the exercise? Do you all remember what it was? Three hundred words on a situation involving war.

It was nice to watch them shuffle, dig in their bags and folders, anticipation gnawing. They were a good bunch that year, even though they weren't the best read; diligent even when given hard work, lively and considerate, a credit to their generation.

—*Sooo*, what have we got? Sam, would you like to start?

—Aw, miss . . .

Hands thrown in the air, forehead touching gray desk. A wrong move, maybe. Didn't want to put him off.

—Thought you said you did it?

—Yeah, but I don't wanna go first.

—*Go on*, I only pick on you cos I know you can take it. I love your work. Be my sacrificial lamb . . .

My miniscule class *ahhed*. Laughter.

—So cute . . . Hayley reached out and rubbed Sam's head. He flinched, fought her off.

—Allow it, man . . .

Trying to sound tough, but I could tell he was pleased.

—Yeah, leave him alone. Sam, would you do the honors?

—Okay . . . He paused, licking his lips. Shall I stan up?

—Sure, why not?

Sam got to his feet.

—This is, like, what I was tryina do, right, was tryina write from the point of view of a guy in Iraq, but I did it in a rhyme. Is dat all right, miss?

—Of course.

—All right . . . It's called "Peace Will Come" . . .

Sam began to sway from side to side, paper in hand, free fingers rigid as though he was about to shake someone's hand, stabbing air. I never understood why the hands were so important when the mouth was doing all the work.

—*In dis peaceless time, I step amongs the grit an the grime, my boots should shine, but I'm jus tryina take care ah mine, the wife an kids, know this is better than a bid, an Hell this is, but I'm jus tryina*

make sure I live, cos true say, where I'm from dat's West London, it's
dog against your own dog, dat's the shit they on, and there's war on
our streets, dat's uncooked beef, and you can see yuh fair share of
distress an da grief, so why stay, let's make hay in a land dat's hot, an
where at least you get paid jus fuh lickin a shot, and who cares who
they are, what they had or they got, or whether it's our own govern-
ment dat's losing the plot, an don't think about the innocents dat die
every night, or if they usin our brawn in a unfair fight, jus put your
head down, brudda, an forget what's right, an think ah video games
when you look down yuh sight . . . Peace . . .

The class erupted, more noise than you would ever
think six teenagers could make, or maybe not if you had
any experience. Sam was grinning while his classmates
slapped his back and clicked their fingers; something I
presumed was the new thing. Heshima was giving Sam
the kind of measured stare the other boys would have
killed for, had they seen it. I clapped with them, trying
not to look too proud. I didn't want to be accused of
favoritism.

—Dat was nice, miss, innit?

Chris, a lean youth the color of hard dough bread,
was grinning, gold tooth catching fluorescent lights.
Gang affiliated, I often thought, probably dealing, had
gold on his fingers, around his neck and his wrists, regularly came in smelling of weed. Never mentioned his
parents, bad sign. If Chris was happy it must have been
good. I'd made the right choice after all.

—It was. That was very good indeed, Sam. I like the
way you got into the head of a man who had a wife and
kids, and the parallels you drew between life here and
the war in Iraq. Very clever. I especially like your character's dilemma. I didn't know if he was right or wrong

at the end, and that's good. Leave moral judgment to the reader, or listener in your case.

—Thanks, miss, I still got more to do though.

—Well, good.

—Man sound like a Yank though, innit, man should spit wid yuh own accent, Jeff said, leaning back on two chair legs, scratching his teeth with a toothpick.

—Shut up!

Heavy emphasis on the *t*, syllables thrown like fists.

—Who you tellin shut up, man?

—You, innit, prick.

—Ay, watch yuh mout, fam . . .

Chair legs slamming, screeching wood. Sam's torso swiveled toward Jeff, who was casual, unafraid. The rest looking elsewhere, especially the girls.

—Hey, hey, what have I said about that type of talk? Any more and you're out, no arguments. Leave it for on the road.

The youths tittered like they always did when I used slang in the wrong syntax. I didn't mind so much. It broke tension. Sam turned around to face me. Jeff sneered.

—Anyone else?

Every hand raised. I breathed out, unable to hide my nerves. Truth be told, my nightmares imagined every day would be that day: when the movies and statistics would be proven right. Nothing had happened in twelve years, but still.

—Go on then, Vanessa.

Her eyes widened. She stood, almost curtsied, trying not to look around the room. Good mother, no dad, kept to herself, fancied by all the boys, couldn't quite make the girls like her as much as I did. Teacher's pet, golden girl, life in a bad area got her in the end. Geared for straight A's, lost confidence and stopped working. Left school with nothing. Happened sometimes.

—I wrote a poem, miss. "Road."

—The stage is yours . . .

Vanessa cleared her throat. The boys had their chins cupped in hands, elbows on desks, smiling, checking out her legs. She tried to ignore them.

—*Harsh streetlight on black tarmac, still night brings no peace. City heartbeat wakes the young, a tattoo calling tattoo-covered strangers out to play new games with new toys, innocent girls and boys lost to ghetto madness, dub plate sadness, no one fearing, hearing, or even listening to the true nature of their environment, stepping closer to their fate, will they escape, or will it be too late? In this, twilight of low insight, low self-esteem, low worth, detached from the realities of earth, no hope of reward or rebirth, is this life or are we cursed? Who knows and so we tread the rocky road, some might stumble, or become humble, some will shoot, shot, or get got, a world made up of kettles and pots, all pointing, all calling, forlorn, forearmed, forewarning, destined to play the same way, heat molded clay to form . . . What? This is less than mere existence, this is life lived to an instant, this is love left by insistence, this is truth told by a brute who doesn't care if you're a yout, fuck being poor, there is more, this is war.*

Harsh intakes of breath. They didn't know how to take it. I tried to hold in my pleasure, was torn between my conflicting desires to congratulate Vanessa and not alienate her further. In the end I couldn't help myself.

—That was wonderful, Vanessa, it really was. Well done. Great wordplay.

—I swore. Sorry, miss.

She collapsed as though her legs had given way. The applause and clicks came late, and they were still looking at her like an alien fallen to earth. Only Hayley was smiling, nodding at Vanessa, making sure she noticed. Sam's brow was furrowed.

—Dat was deep. Intense.

I wasn't sure whether he was being complimentary or not, so I moved on.

—Any more?

No hands. After a beat, Jeff raised his. My mental groan was so loud for a moment I actually thought I'd heard it. I forced a smile.

—Jeff. Got one about Tupac?

—Yeah, miss, how d'you know?

Grinning, standing, paper in hand, brash confidence and posturing. The class in noisy uproar.

—Cos you always write about Tupac, innit! Heshima shouted. She had a loud voice, probably due to living with four older brothers, the reason why, as pretty as she was, no one went near her.

—Man's like he's in love, fam . . . Sam put one hand on his heart. *Tupac . . . Biggie . . . They were friends ah mine . . . We want you to know . . . That we love you so . . .* he sang, deliberately off-key, oblivious to the glare Jeff bored into the back of his head.

—Shut the fuck up, bruv . . .

—Man as t'do better to stop man . . .

—Hey! Last time, I'm telling you.

—Sorry, miss, man, but can you tell him?

—Sam, let him have his say, will you? He can't help being emotional, love's a very strong feeling.

They screamed, slapped tables, thighs. Jeff gave me

the Medusa stare. Whoops. Definitely the wrong move. Even Chris was sniggering. Jeff sat down.

—Jeff, I'm sorry. That was a joke, all right? I shouldn't have said it. Jeff, please stand up.

—Nah, miss.

Sullen, lips pouted.

—Please, Jeff, I apologize, it was wrong.

—Nah, man.

Chris elbowed his friend. Sniggering went off like firecrackers.

—Go on, fam, don't be like dat. Man can't take a joke?

—Nah, I ain doin nuttin.

Chris kept goading, kept trying. The wait felt like hours. I let it ride, tried to get the class to calm down. Jeff eventually got to his feet, dramatizing the decision, half-crouched like an old man.

—No laughin or nuttin, all right?

—Absolutely. No laughing. Not a word.

I shot a look at everyone to make sure, face set. Sam winked. I could have killed him, though I managed not to smile.

—All yours, Jeff.

He was grinning again, back straight, bad boy posture returned.

—All right, people, dis one's called "R.I.P." He rattled paper, stood as tall as his squat frame allowed. *When Tupac died* . . .

Jeff stopped, looked around. Heshima was shaking, face red, pretty lips pursed. Vanessa was eyeballing a corner of the room, one hand covering her mouth. Sam gave me a wide grin while the others rolled on their desks. It was all the class could do not to erupt in laughter. I had to smile, even as I fought against it; luckily, it seemed Jeff had finally caught on. He nodded, lip curled at the edges as if to say he knew he was funny, but now he had created the joke. He turned back to his paper.

—*When Tupac died he knew the world was as fucked up as they said, cos it was like dat around his way too, an people died every day, an his cousin had been stabbed to deat when he was fourteen, so didn't dat prove it was always dat way? He blazed* All Eyez on Me *until his sister screamed at him, den he screamed back before he went out, cos he couldn't take her shit no more. He took his shank cos he was supposed to meet his bredrin on Oxford Street, outside JD Sports. For some reason his bredrin never turned up, so when the businessman pushed him as he got on the bus on his way home, he didn't think, he just used it—four quick stabs—and watched him fall to the ground bleeding all over. He got on the train and was back around his way in half an hour, scared but unable to admit it, an when Crackhead Winnie asked him fuh a score he nearly shanked him too—but held it down, telling the cat to piss off and trouble someone else.* Long pause, eyeballing the room. *When Biggie died he said fuck it, got himself a gun.*

Jeff grinned, sat down. The applause was measured. I hoped it would go on for a while, wasn't surprised when it didn't. The kids wore mute faces, no flicker of smiles. Chris clapped his friend on the shoulder, proud.

—Right . . . Not from personal experience, I hope?

—Nah, miss. What I see, y'get me?

—Right. Deep breath. Okay, class, any more contenders?

There were not. When the silence stretched long enough I gave them the printouts, copies of Raymond

Carver's "The Father," and had Vanessa read. I liked her voice; it was clear and strong, unflavored by the coarse street accent most of the kids adopted. I don't know where that accent came from, it was flavored neither by African, West Indian, nor English pronunciation, and occurred no matter the race of the speaker—a guttural rasp, a lowering of tone that made me cringe despite myself, made me want to shake them and ask whether they were taught to speak English properly.

Vanessa was different. A distant cousin to those working-class sons and daughters, she was of their world but not from it, and it showed. When she finished the Carver excerpt there was more applause, immediate and honest. She lowered her head and blushed. We talked about the author, where he came from and what he'd written about, then the piece itself, which had quieted most of the bravado, even from the boys. I allowed myself a mental pat on the back. Another clincher. Even Jeff was joining the conversation, looking at me with sincerity mapped in his stoned eyes, with respect.

That made me think. The boy beneath the Westway, the staring, him following. I don't know why, but the more I looked at my kids the more the idea grew, solidified into reason. It struck me dead, feet encased, mind lost, until I remembered where I was, that I had to teach.

I asked them to start on their own writing, keeping it loose—something, anything, about a father or father figure in their own lives, fictionalized to make it interesting. I promised I'd be calling on the ones who got away without reading next week, which made Sam look up at me, grateful, and that was it. Another two hours gone like minutes. I slow-walked to the door, reluctant to leave our group warmth for the cold ambiguity of night. Sam was by my side as usual, and Hayley; both youths often accompanied me home. I watched Vanessa leave alone, thinking I'd walk with her next time, making that mental note.

Outside, the others loitered around Jeff, bouncing on toes, hoods raised, avoiding my eyes. Smoking was on the cards, or so it seemed. I ducked my head, continued home with Sam and Hayley on either side.

⤳

The word pain comes from the Latin *poena*, meaning penalty or fine.

⤳

People also say time is relative, a point with which I agree. As invisible to the naked eye as oxygen, or indeed pain, time as experienced by human beings has the amazing ability to occur simultaneously in the past, present, and future. Everything on the planet, from the tiniest amoeba to humankind, has been, is being, and will also become. It's almost too fascinating for words. That we exist cocooned within an unseen element shifting faster than we can comprehend, that no sooner than we enter the present it is already the past and we are always, without pause or hesitation, speeding full throttle toward the future, is as mind-boggling as the thought that we are standing on a tilted spinning rock that orbits alongside seven other tilted spinning rocks, all circling a gigantic ball of gas that burns from the inside out.

Ponder this. If I lift my finger and touch the end of my nose, I am touching my nose in the present, have touched my nose in the past, and am also, and always will be, about to lower my finger from my nose in the future. Each possibility is as real as the other and all exist at once, or none at all. The moment I touch my nose, I have touched my nose, and will cease touching my nose. Like I said, fascinating.

Is there a point to all this? Of course. There is always a point. What I mean is this journal is as fixed to time as time is to me—that it exists in three planes because that is the nature of things; and I'm a stickler for nature. Give me my meat organic, hold the GM. So if my writing exists on three planes—past, present, and future—please don't be afraid. I'll probably keep future to a minimum because at this point it's dark and damp and it scares me, but I can't guarantee anything. Que sera, sera. Let the chips fall as they may. It is what it is.

⤳

Who am I?

- My name is Beverley Rachel Cottrell
- I am forty-six years old
- I am a teacher
- I am a homeowner
- I am an orphan
- I am a sister
- I am a mother
- I am a divorcée
- I am a lover

- I am a mental patient
- I am a murderer
- I am alone
- I am anger

⤸

I woke up to heat. Real, unfettered heat. Though my blanket was thin I could feel damp on my skin, on my top lip, between my legs. *Urrrgh.* I opened my eyes and stretched and when the soles of my feet hit the bottom of the bed, it shocked me. I felt a scratchy sensation, a rasp, and I *knew*, instantly mind you, that the soles were hard. That was the second shock, though it wasn't my last.

I sat up and took a look around. My room was tiny; the walls bare wood painted white a long time ago, now peeling. My bed was tiny. There was a trunk at the bottom of the bed that was blue and battered and the locks were rusting and guess what—yep, that was tiny too. A red and black rug woven from rough cotton lay on the bare wooden floor. Frilled dresses hung from nails in the wooden walls; a window just above the railed headboard spilt a beam of morning light; a large, broken shard of mirror, dusted with tiny orange spots, stood against the wall where the dresses were. In the corner of the room there was a large web, and a large, long-legged black spider sat in the middle.

I slipped from the bedsheet and placed my hard feet on the warm floorboards. The skinny brown legs that emerged told me everything, and the pink hem of my nightie, and the red and black cotton bracelet around my wrist, but I had to look, I had to make sure. I tottered over to the shard of mirror, weak at the knees, still sleepy, until I was staring at my reflection.

I was around nine years old. Brown pigtails and big eyes. Yellow as a daffodil. Gaps in my teeth when I bared them. Dressed in a pink cotton nightie that reached my ankles.

And it was *hot* like hellfire.

I smelled something nice, realized it was coming from outside of my room. Slowly, like I was sleepwalking, I placed one foot before the other, opened my bedroom door, and stepped into the corridor. I could hear a rhythmic banging from somewhere in the house, a steady dull clang. I saw the image of a huge, dark-skinned man, shirtsleeves rolled to his elbows. Couldn't stop walking. My nose was raised. The smell was overpowering, sugar and milk and goodness. I walked, oblivious to blank white doors, following the smell to the kitchen. There was a woman, seemingly tall as the ceiling, wearing a long denim dress with no sleeves and a plain red cloth that covered her hair, stirring a massive pot of cornmeal porridge. I saw and dismissed the black letters on her upper shoulder, raised lumps writhing in time with her movements. She was about to cut banana slices into the pot when she felt my presence, I suppose, because she turned.

She was beautiful. Lemon-slice eyes, bright gray, almost silver, lean face, and angular cheekbones. She opened her arms to greet me.

"Good morning, sugar pie."

Her voice was as sweet as the odor of porridge. I ran to her and threw myself into the rough folds of her dress and kissed her.

"Beverley? Beverley, why are you cryin?"

"Mi nuh know, Muma . . ."

I heard a thud deep within my skull. White light exploded. My head rocked backward. Mama was suddenly glaring, hand poised.

"What did I say? What did I say about talking like that?"

My lip trembled. I looked into eyes that had turned from silver to dark gray like storm clouds. Her face was red.

"Mi—" I took a pause, tried again. "I don't know Mama."

"You mustn't talk like those field hands, not now, not ever. Do you hear?"

My head was low. Mucus formed inside my nose.

"Yes, Mama."

Tears splashed the dusty wooden floor.

"Oh, baby . . ."

Her arms enfolded me and I buried my head in her dress. I felt comforted, even though I knew I shouldn't.

"Mama's sorry she lost her temper. Do you forgive me?"

I nodded, rubbing a dark trail of mucus against denim. That would teach her.

"Okay." Raising my chin, touching my forehead with soft lips. "Go and get your sister for breakfast."

I turned, leaving the room without looking back. There was something in the way Mama breathed that let me know she was watching me, and my walk was stiff-legged all the way. The clanging was still going on; in fact, it had grown louder. *Clang. Clang. Clang.* Coming from behind one of those doors, but I didn't want to see. The noise scared me. The whole house did.

It took a long time to decide which door to pick. There were three in the corridor, lined up like playing cards, my open bedroom door at the end. I didn't want to open the wrong one and expose the cause of the clang. I didn't know why. I waited with my eyes closed until Mama called my name. Eyes squeezed tight, I stepped forward and knocked on the door beside mine.

"Come!"

I turned the dented brass knob. The room was bigger than mine, covered in pink—everything from the bedsheets and pillows to the see-through cloth on the wooden wardrobe. The fluffy rug on the floor and flowers entwined by thin stems that arced across the window frame. A tall girl of around fourteen was standing by the window, back to me. I didn't even know her name. I went inside.

"Uh . . . Mama say come for breakfast."

"I'm comin," she said, but didn't move.

I joined her by the windowsill, had to stand on tiptoes. Blue skies and a vast abundance of trees in the distance, a hill of some kind, a towering wall of green. Birds shooting past at high speed. A constant hum of insects. I heard a scratching noise and looked closer to home. An old man swept the grass in the yard, his movements limited and stiff. He was collecting fallen leaves, although his focus was not on the work. He was looking at us, through the window and into my sister's room, his eyes yellow like a cat.

"They hate us."

I turned to my sister. Her head was propped on her hands, and her dark pigtails shone, a black that almost matched her skin. She smelled of sweet perfume. Her eyes were long-lashed, stunning, half closed as though she was dreaming. I loved her, felt the emotion rush into my body, making my blood fizz.

"Why?"

"Because they think we hate them."

The old man was still there, jaw moving. If it wasn't for that and the movement of his hands, I might have thought he'd been carved, stood in the yard for our benefit.

"Do we?"

Everything shifted. I found myself in the kitchen looking down on my bowl of cornmeal porridge, taking a huge spoonful into my mouth, smarting at the heat. My nameless sister sat across the table from me, eating and not looking at anyone. Mama was to my right and on my left there was the huge man, leather dark, wearing dungarees and a white shirt, sleeves rolled up to the elbows. He ate porridge as though there was a contest, fast and formidable, spoon scraping against his bowl. Everyone ignored him. I couldn't help but watch. He turned and peered at me, a strong handsome face, something in the eyes that reminded me of my sister, which made sense I suppose. They did look alike, but it wasn't that. It was their dreamy gaze, as though they were someplace else.

"Lovely morning."

Mama's voice, light, chin raised, head rigid. Papa lifted his eyes to the window for a split second, returned to his bowl.

"Did you finish the McIntyre order?"

I looked from one to the other. Kicked my feet.

"Mi soon done."

I saw Mama try not to wince. Wondered if she ever slapped him. She avoided my eyes.

"They're getting quite testy about the whole thing. Second time they've been back."

"Mi say mi soon done."

Firm. Spoon resting against the edge of the bowl, elbows on the table. I could see dust twirl in the light from the window like a minuscule ballet.

"Beverley, stop kicking."

Mama put her hand on mine. I stopped, looked at Papa. He tried to smile. Saw my sister gazing into space and the muscles that propped up his lips collapsed. He looked into his porridge bowl. Mama took her hand from mine, put it on his. I missed the soft feel of her fingers. My sister began to kick her feet.

I felt that shift again and I was standing behind a shop counter, the bridge of my nose meeting the edge of cool, rough wood, just about able to see. Mama sat on a stool beside me knitting with two pale cream needles, humming under her breath. I stood on tiptoes. Mama saw my efforts and smiled. I grinned back, breath hissing through missing teeth like a penny whistle, tried again. If I found purchase with my toes, I could pull myself up onto the counter. I could see.

Over the counter edge, a smell of dry wood filling my nostrils, rows of metal chains hung from the ceiling. The omega of wrist and ankle shackles. The long, barbed ends of neck braces. Cat-o'-nines made from rope, leather, metal. The blunt, square ends of branding irons. Ankle chains forged to metal balls. I saw padlocks, and keys, which I discovered housed in a rack on top of the counter, not far from the embossed silver till.

The world beyond our shop counter had turned to dull metal. I let go, dropped to the floor. My legs gave way.

I felt Mama rush to my side, though I couldn't see her, felt her warm hands as she lifted me to my feet.

"Be careful, *cherie*, you must watch what you do . . ."

I nodded, no voice in my throat, gazing into Mama's eyes. Their glint was not unlike the chains.

The shop bell rang. The noise of the outside world grew louder for a moment, birdsong and the hum of insects accompanied by men's voices engaged in discussion, lowering as the door closed. Mama let me go so quick I almost fell again, got to her feet, knees popping like twigs underfoot. There was a steady thud of steps coming toward the counter but I couldn't see whom they belonged to. I hopped, skipped, and jumped to the right, unsteady on my legs. I unlocked the hook of the gate, pushed.

The man wore dark work trousers, heavy black boots, a white shirt damp with sweat. He seemed tall enough for the crown of his head to brush the rafters, and made Mama appear small beside him. His face was red, glistening. He dabbed at his forehead with a handkerchief, winked in my direction. Leaned across the counter.

"Mornin, Maggie."

"Mr. McIntyre . . ."

Big, red-faced smile.

"Darlin, I've told youse you can call us Nick . . ."

"Of course. Are you well?"

"All the better for seein you."

Firm pressure. It took seconds to realize I was frowning.

"Thank you." Mama's voice had that feather-light

feel, laced with something else, some distant tremor. I slid behind the counter to join her. Her hand descended onto my head, but she never took her eyes away from the man she called Mr. McIntyre. "Now, how can I help, Nick? I assume you've come about the replacements?"

"You assume correct."

"Let me get Shane." Mama turned toward the white door behind the counter, called into the house. McIntyre reached for the mounted padlocks and keys next to the till, lifted one from the rack, and slipped it somewhere I couldn't see, below the counter. His pocket, I presumed. I opened my mouth to tell Mama, when he smiled, put his finger to his lips, wagged it slowly from side to side. I looked at the floorboards. Mama rejoined my side. "He won't be a minute, Nick."

It had to be less than fifteen seconds before Papa came through the shop door wielding a crate that made his forearms bulge. He gasped as he placed it on the counter. Dust puffed when it landed. I glanced up at my father and the dreamy gaze was gone. In fact, I had never seen such focus. It was as though there was no one left in the universe besides Papa and McIntyre. I looked from one to the other and even though McIntyre was smiling, I was scared.

"Mornin."

"Mornin, Missa McIntyre."

"These things fixed now, boy?"

"Yes, baas, dem fix good. De screw rust, but mi replace dem. Dem nuh trouble yu again."

"Better not." McIntyre was thumbing greasy notes. He laid them on the counter. "I'm keepin twenty percent. For time wasted."

Papa made to say something. I saw Mama clasp his hand beneath the counter, squeeze, and realized how much she looked like the version of myself I'd seen in the mirror. Papa nodded.

"Yes, baas."

"Good. Bring my goods to the cart, would you?"

I almost gasped. McIntyre's thin mouth was open, and sweat dotted his upper lip as he watched my father. There was an empty space that should have been filled with words. I waited, but nothing happened. Beneath the counter, Papa's forearm bulged. His fist was clenched so tight the tendons were jumping. "Shane?"

"Yes, baas."

I heard myself exhale. Papa's fingers unraveled, reaching for the crate. He lifted with a grunt and followed three paces in McIntyre's shadow, walking to the door. The bell rattled, raucous in the silence of the hot store, ushering the outside in.

❧

Repairs to be made:

- Call electrician about bathroom light cord
- And broken plug socket in bedroom
- Buy bleach for bathroom sink
- Call housing association about skirting board
- Replace various small bulbs
- Reaffix loose tile
- Replace battery in door bell
- Replace battery in fire alarm

❦

A fairy-tale orange glow, the glistening damp of pavement attempting to shine despite the grime and candy wrappers and muck-coated surfaces. Real life. A bummer. I walked with Hayley and Sam, hearing them speak, not listening. What I felt was far from hope, but it was some form of awareness. The feeling of being stalked, almost hunted, had woken me from my stupor, had made my fingers tingle and my breathing loud in my ears. I took close note of the tiny things in life, like the rub of clothes against my skin, and was grateful.

I could feel him. Obviously that sounds illogical, the benefit of hindsight rather than anything I know, but I remember the thought clearly, as if it had been spoken; the tall boy would not go away. I would see him again, the sneer, the lazy walk, and it would continue until we spoke. This I knew, though I would not admit it. He was coming. Why, I didn't know. How, I hoped to find out. But the tall boy seeing me was no coincidence. Neither was the fact that he knew where I lived. It might have been the first time I had noticed him, but this boy had been watching me. For how long, I didn't know. There were many reasons, many possibilities, and I refused to consider the biggest, the most earth shattering, until I learned more. He would have to find me, but I would be waiting.

Every shadow wore his certainty. Every sound, every movement was the boy emerging from darkness, flooded by overhead lighting. My kids noticed the silence but were kind enough to leave me be, walked me home believing they were doing right. I wasn't sure. He was there, I could feel him, but he wouldn't make an appearance while they were with me. I wanted to tell them, considered it the whole way, and decided against it. Hayley was harmless enough. Sam too, actually, but they both knew people who lived to cause harm. If they took things the way I had, focused on the negative, there could be the type of violence I was trying to curb. It was all gangs and territories for miles around. So I kept my mouth shut, hugged and wished them well until next week, let myself into the building. All the way to my door I expected to turn a corner and find him, but no one was there.

I heated dinner, wandered from room to room. I was restless, didn't know what to do with myself. I was excited. I was waiting. I went back into the kitchen and saw a Post-it on my fridge door, curled, hanging by a corner. It said: *Don't eat the strawberry pie three days in a row.*

I smiled. Though I had no intention of doing so, the note was comforting. I looked further, past wrinkled postcards and champagne bottle magnets. There were a few more. I chose.

The life cocooned is not your own.

I frowned, inspected the note like overripe fruit. Picked. Tore it in half and threw it into the trash, followed by the one about strawberry pie. Relished the satisfying clang. Like Papa and his god-awful workshop. I reminded myself I had to tell Sue.

There were more Post-it notes in the kitchen drawer, bags of them. I peeled one from an open pack, wrote: *Don't sleep with Seth. Ever.* I took the note into the bedroom and stuck it on the headboard where I could see it, lay on the bed. I put my feet up.

∽

How strange that I sit in darkness, and only now do I see.

∽

I'm pretty sure he came that night. I slept in the living room, where I could hear, and around two in the morning there was a shuffling outside my door, then the letter box opened and I could tell someone was looking in, though I couldn't see their eyes, just hear them. Whoever it was had a cold, a runny nose, so they had to inhale through their mouth and they kept wiping at it. I don't even know why I keep saying *they*, no one else would have been peering through my letter box at two a.m., not even Seth; it was the tall boy, I knew.

Once he'd got up his courage the boy started knocking really loud, and when that didn't work, he rang the bell. I wanted to go and see, but to be honest I was still scared. I was a woman alone and answering the door at that hour in a neighborhood like mine was against the rules. So I sat with my blanket under my chin and listened to him knock until one of the guys from a few flats down came out. I heard voices and my late-night visitor's feet take him away, back down the stairs, onto the street.

∽

That morning, getting ready, I found another Post-it on the side of my bathtub, one I'd forgotten. It said: *If you don't like hot water, keep a close eye on your bath.* I thought that was quite profound.

❧

I took my Honda instead of the bus and drove over Harrow Road into Kensal Rise. Sue and her partner had a nice semidetached they'd bought awhile ago, or it had been in the family, something like that. The traffic was light and I made good time.

Howard, Sue's partner, let me into a bare hallway, white walls and no furniture, ghostly dust sheets draped on banisters. He smiled at my surprise.

—Redecorating, he told me. Go on up.

I followed carpetless stairs. There was a small corridor, some doors, the anorexic wooden chair. I sat and gazed at white walls. Voices came from beyond the door, Sue's office. Before long I heard a rustle of movement, a creak of floorboards, the low groan of an opening door.

—Have a good day, Sue told the man. His eyes were fixed on his feet.

—Cheerio, he said, thundering down the bare wooden staircase.

—Beverley, wonderful to see you, on time as usual.

—Hi, Sue, I said, standing. I do try.

The office wasn't really one. A small room with a filing cabinet, a table with a few leaflets, some copies of *CPR* and *Grief Digest*. In the early days Sue had tried to palm me off with an issue of the grief magazine, but when I said I'd rather slit my wrists, she stopped. Two chairs faced each other as though deep in conversation: Sue's high-back, classy leather and a smaller, squatter version with thin armrests. There were faded abstract prints on two of the four walls. It was the only decorated room I'd seen.

We got comfortable, smiled a lot.

—You're redecorating, Howard tells me?

—Yes, it's more than about time. Our youngest just left for uni, so . . . Sue smiled, trailed off.

I didn't mind, though I was conscious of people thinking I might. Life went on. I didn't expect everybody to pretend they didn't have children.

—Exciting times. Must feel like your life is your own.

—Yes, that's exactly it. I've wanted to fix the place up for ages, and Howard's not much of a DIY person, but he's an able enough assistant, so I tend to strip and refill, he paints and repaints. Worked out quite well and we've saved a bundle.

—It really brings out the character of the place. You have a beautiful home.

Sue nodded, she knew it was true. She also knew my old house had been quite similar. I'd shown her pictures. It seemed every time I opened my mouth, the past I tried so hard to force down came leapfrogging out, squat and ugly, croaking on the floor between us. I didn't mean it that way, it just was.

Sue shifted in the silence and leather groaned, as if making a point.

—So, anything to tell?

—Lots.

She motioned with her hand, a gentle push.

—Go ahead.

—Well, I've been having the dream.

—Barbados?

—Yes.

—And you're a slave?

—No. I smiled. I think it's the slavery era, but it seems like I'm free. Feels like I'm free anyway.

—That's right. Your family sells products of slavery to plantation owners?

Nicely put, I thought. Products of slavery.

—Yes.

—Any changes?

—Well, this time I had a sister.

—Jackie was in your dream?

—No, it wasn't her. I never found out her name. She was older than me, and very pretty. She looked like my father.

—Your real father, the one you saw in the first dreams? Who made the products?

—Yes, he made the shackles and chains.

I waited.

—Hmmm . . . So what was she like?

—Very quiet. Sad.

—Why?

—They hated us. The other Africans, they hated us for what we were doing. And then I saw a man come into our store and belittle my father in front of my mother. He was flirting with her before my father came, and when their backs were turned, he stole a padlock. I saw him, but I didn't say anything. My father hated him worse than anything but he had to take the man's orders. I was scared.

—Because your father wouldn't back down?

—Yes. You had to back down or die.

—Even a big, strong man like him?

—Yes. Those were the rules.

Sue nodded.

—So your mother and father were the mother and father you had, and your sister was some random, fictitious character?

—Yes.

—Isn't that strange?

—Very.

—Any idea why you would dream something like that?

—Isn't this the part where you tell me?

We laughed. Sue rocked, held her stomach, and closed her eyes. I think she was putting it on, but that's just me.

—Only joking. Yes, I think I know. I paused. This still feels stupid. Saying.

—Try.

—I could write it much better.

—I think you should say it. See how it feels.

I blew out a long breath, sagged.

—Okay. I think I feel guilty.

—Because of your sense of privilege?

I gave Sue a grateful smile.

—Exactly. I think I go to the club, and I hear these kids talk and listen to their lives and I realize just how much my parents shielded me. How much stock they put into books, leading by example, into sports and education and just being there. I always took what they did for granted; it's what you were supposed to do, right? Your duty as a parent. But now I think differently. God, I feel differently.

Sue leaned forward, serious.

—You don't know that your family was involved in the slave trade.

—We've been wealthy for generations. My dream sister was dark, and my whole family are as light as me. Especially my real sister. You don't get either way in the Caribbean without a bit of dabbling.

—Fair point. But that's the past isn't it? What can you do?

—I don't know. I'm hoping I'll find out and stop dreaming about them. It's annoying.

—I can imagine it is. She sat back, assessed me. Now Beverley, I have a question. You don't have to answer. I'm just wondering how much of a role you feel Malakay plays in these dreams, as an actual physical presence or in their formulation?

I opened my mouth. The words weren't there. I knew what I wanted to say, what was being said in my mind, but it wouldn't emerge from my throat. I started to grow hot, and it wasn't fear or nerves that made that happen, it was excitement.

—I saw him.

Sue struggled to keep her face rigid. I could see the twitch, her reaction. Slight, but I caught it.

—You mean you saw him in your dream . . .

—No, in real life. Clear as sunshine.

—Is that possible?

—Yes. I saw him.

—In real life . . .

—I think so. A boy about the age Malakay would be followed me from Portobello Market to my house. He was there when I walked home from the club, and last night he knocked at my door. It was Malakay. I recognized him.

A moment, where she gauged what she was going to say, watched my every move. When she spoke, it was a slow release of words, soft as a whisper, easily snatched back if chosen unwisely.

—Have you called the police?

—No . . . I was thinking I'd wait . . .

Shaking her head, fidgeting in the classy seat that groaned with her movements.

—You should call and report it, just in case.

—Sue . . . look, I know what this seems like. I felt the same when I saw him, I ran like hell. I've been thinking ever since, and it's the only thing that makes sense. I looked into his face, into his eyes, and even though I didn't want to believe it, I saw my son. I know.

—But . . . Sitting up in her chair. The last time you saw him he was eight months old. You couldn't possibly recognize him.

—Who else would do that?

—One of your kids.

—It wasn't them.

—One of their friends, maybe, someone who knows your background? Some young man who has the hots for you, or heard about the terrific work you're doing? You can't assume it was your son based on absolutely nothing . . .

—I feel it. Here.

I touched my heart, didn't regret it, even as I saw the look on her face. Regression. Sue thinking I'd been climbing so well, now this.

—Beverley. Let me speak as a friend. We've known each other long enough, right? You're a smart woman. I know it's hard to hear, but the likelihood of that child being yours is so slim that it doesn't bear thinking. I'd hate to see you hurt.

Her eyes were so sincere they pushed me toward laughter. I fought it down, knowing how *that* would look.

—It's what the dream meant. I should be mindful of my past. My conditioning. I need to unlearn.

Sue took my hand between hers. She bent over, back hunched, until I raised my head.

—This is dangerous, Beverley. In every way. I want you to promise you'll be sensible.

I was smiling so hard my jaws hurt. I squeezed Sue's hand.

—You'll see. One day I'll tell you what happened, and you'll be glad because I was right. You'll see.

Sue let go, turned away.

❧

We talked about Jackie and the after-school kids and then the hour was done. I could tell Sue was shaken by what I had said, yet I felt giddy, alive. She walked me to the front door, down the creaking stairs, across the echoing passage, nodding as if she heard what I was saying, miles away. She clutched my shoulder with fingers like the sallow flesh of raw chicken wings, held me.

—You know you needn't see me anymore. There hasn't been cause for years.

—I like the company, I said, and gave her a hug.

❧

Pain is perceived in the cortex, and plays an important role in the lives of humans and animals, helping them to function normally. Some people feel no pain. This is rare, but there are cases of people who can break their own bones and feel nothing. The disorder is known as congenital insensitivity.

❦

The perfect day smiled down on me as I drove toward home. The skies, although far from empty, were stark blue and the clouds were cream gray and white like the bellies of thoroughbred birds. I thought about warm, soft feathers. Of flight and the vast emptiness above my head. I thought about my conversation with Sue, how such little things could set off such emotion. One boy, one glance, and everything had changed. Only days before, my mind had felt like a void, now it was filled with practicalities, suspicion, nervous energy, and hope. I bit my lip often, to keep from smiling.

When I pulled up outside my block I saw a figure, back turned, moving from side to side. Sweeping. I parked and the figure swung around, waved. Ida.

I joined her, eyes dancing just in case he was there. I wanted to let him know it was okay. I wasn't scared. I'd made a knee-jerk mistake. I didn't intend to let some random kid from the street enter my home in the thick of night, but if I saw him now I would speak to him. I wasn't sure how to inform him of my new resolution, although I thought it best that I saw him before he saw me. Ida continued to sweep, until I got close. She stood, held her hip. Leaned back.

—Afternoon, love.

—Afternoon, Ida. You okay?

—I am. Swishing night-before rubbish into a mounting pile by her feet, rhythmic, repetitive work. Heard that racket over yours. Who was knocking so late?

—I'm not sure, that's why I didn't answer. Sorry.

—Some bloke, Downie reckons. Young fella.

—I see, I said.

She caught my expressionless, closed-mouth face, swept harder.

—You read the leaflets they put through our doors? About the meters?

—Yes, I did.

The council had been threatening to install parking meters on our little cul-de-sac for years. It had always been residential permits only, but now the addition of paid parking meant we would be competing for vehicle space with the tourists and visitors. I sighed, looked around.

—Well, I suppose it was inevitable.

—I know it was, but I don't see why they shouldn't concern themselves with spending money on community safety. I mean, look at that.

Ida pointed her broom high on the opposite wall. The CCTV camera, a limp, broken limb, filming the sidewalk, jerking fitfully. I tutted.

—Can you believe it?

—Wouldn't be so bad, if it wasn't for that.

Ida swung her broom 180 degrees toward the street end of the block. A group of kids, some standing with hoods up, others on bikes, feet poised, ready to take off. I counted six, had seen them as I pulled onto my street, but was so used to ignoring their presence they'd hardly registered. Most were tall and broad as the boy, hulking from here to there, restless. Loud voices and laughter, puffs of smoke. Blue language, staccato words in time with the mechanical jerk of the camera, chopping hands. Expression as combat. Tongue-fu. Most seemed consumed by what the rapper was saying, apart from one kid who dwarfed his bike, gray hood turned our way. Grime Reaper. We noticed each other, a trio of sight lines converging, and then I dropped my head, turned back to the building, saw Ida's head already down, hands sweeping.

—Out there every night they are.

—I know, Ida.

—Selling drugs, drinking, messing with young girls.

—We don't know they're dealing. They could be hanging out.

—Why don't they hang out inside? In your club, they could go there.

—There's nothing for them, Ida. I teach creative writing of sorts, and if they've no interest there's nothing. I mean, the center has lots of activities but no money to do the stuff they'd really like . . .

—So we have to put up with them? Their rubbish and filthy talk . . .

—I know, Ida. I just don't think anyone's going to come and clear this up for us.

Ida sighed, stopped sweeping. Looked at me properly.

—They didn't want people like you living here, not so long ago.

—I remember.

—It was the same then. Different, but the same. You understand?

—I think so. You survived though.

Ida touched the pile of trash with her brush.

—I think I'll bake. Would you like dessert?

—Yes, please.

—Pecan pie, maybe?

—That would be lovely. Do you need ingredients, or do you have everything?

—Some pecans is all.

—I'll go to the shops. I patted my pockets as Ida dug into hers. I'll get it, don't worry. See you in a bit.

—See you, love.

I walked to the end of the block. Grime Reaper watched. I kept my head straight, on the road, ignored him until he lost interest. That satisfied me for some reason.

ல்

If time is the master, who is the mistress?

ல்

There is the matter of what happened, and how, and when, and of course my own shirking of details, which is understandable, I'm sure. I'm not going to go into a diatribe about the whole awfulness, how hard it is to look back, all that angst. But I can say this—since the moment I started writing I knew I had to get to this point, the part where I tell. It seems my life ever since has been a constant debate of do I, don't I, are they worthy, should I let things be? It's the constant murmur in the back of my class, the one I try to dismiss and always fail to.

So, on with the show.

I can't recount what happened verbatim because I don't actually know. It was him. My husband. Reduce anything to a simple noun and it's easy to retain distance. Let's make things tougher, shall we? Let's call him Patrick. That was his name, and it's his story, so we should at least call him by it. Patrick. There was a time when I loved the sound those combined syllables made.

Patrick was taking care of Malakay because I had gone back to my workplace to talk about my return from maternity leave. I was reluctant to be away from my child, but I didn't want to leave the job for too long. We weren't rich enough not to need the money, and my maternity benefits only went so far. I'd ordered a few bottles of milk and left them in the fridge with carrot slices, as Malakay liked them to chew on and was just becoming aware of solids. Patrick was taking our son to Ravenscourt Park so he could crawl in the grass and get some fresh air—*Daddy too*, I remember thinking. That much I know.

From what I have been told, Patrick did go to the park early that morning, stayed until lunchtime, and left. He was feeling peckish so he stopped at a Chinese takeout, as our cupboards at home were bare. I'd taken to advance cooking, big batches, sometimes three pots on the go, cooled and placed in the freezer. Malakay was sleeping badly and I suppose I was nervous about my job, because I hadn't found time to cook that week, and that's what plagued me terribly over the years, the thought that had I been a better wife, more committed, less caught up with my career, I never would have lost my son. No matter how ludicrous the thought, it exists, even as I write.

So Patrick stopped outside the takeout, and you might be thinking he immediately unbuckled Malakay and brought our child with him, but he did not. He was inside for twenty minutes ordering chicken fried rice and chili prawn balls. When he came out, Malakay was gone. Nothing else was taken from the locked car, just our child.

And that's it. That simple. One minute I was an ordinary mother, doing ordinary motherly things, next I was some red-faced, claw-fingered monster with leaking eyes and bad skin, a tendency to scratch like a kitten, leaping at things, people, casting them aside, Patrick most of all. I just couldn't, *can't* understand what he had done to me. How he had managed to return without searching every street and alley of this stinking city that swallowed my son; every car, every person, every home and public space. The worst thing was my coming home knowing nothing, spying the police outside my house and rushing inside to see him sitting there, head bowed, two officers on either side like bookends, crying into his mug of tea and not looking at me while *they* told me, it was them who had the guts, and even when I asked where this had happened I could see it, the white plastic bag that contained the greasy, rotten food this man had forsaken my son for, and I couldn't help myself, I just grabbed it, and swung it, and hit him full in the face, and I kept hitting until the cheap, nasty food tumbled from the bag, and the policemen held my arms and wrestled me to the floor, and I was sick everywhere and I've never eaten Chinese since.

After that, it was all familiar. Police reports, separate rooms, and separate accounts. Phone calls received and made. Our dog Caesar, snout on paws, overshadowed by suffering. Flowers, cards, food arriving on our doorstep, forlorn faces, family. Camped by the phone, one wife and her husband, together and apart. No news, a few rumors, nothing concrete. Us sitting behind a long wooden table, police banners in front and behind like some football stadium, jugs of water and glasses and microphones and thick black cables. Patrick gazing into space, me holding the handwritten note I couldn't read when the time came because my fingers were trembling, my voice was trembling, I was trembling all over and I could taste my own grief, bitter grit. Jackie and Frank in the wings like understudies, early days for them and what a thing to happen while they were still dating, what a thing to remember when people asked, *How did you two meet?* When your honeymoon period is synonymous with the worst pain in family history, why wouldn't you wave that goodbye, retreat into your own shell, lest you become infected with the compound known as loss?

Another baby-snatch from a South London hospital a month after, horror that a mother might endure my pain. Patrick and I together on the sofa, cordless on my lap, watching the news. Day after day. Each an agonizing stretch of what if they're linked, there's a pattern, a nursery of stolen babies locked in a basement, kept in the dark for reasons we dare not think about. Then seventeen days later, a return. The cherubic baby found in the Cotswolds with a bogus health worker, celebration. Our excitement, a vague sense of fear. It had been forty-seven days for us.

The police at our door, unsmiling. Patrick hauled away in cuffs, telling me to call the partners. The news reports that evening, after I spent all day at the station, saying he had been arrested, not charged, for questioning. The tense, stoic faces in my home, my mother without makeup, my father's worry forming deep crevices, no one talking, no one meeting my eyes, no one able to say much of anything, avoiding any mention of Patrick, keeping their eyes away from the candles and trinkets surrounding pictures of my son. I would commune with him alone, I would bow my head and weep and pray. I would look into his gentle eyes and curse myself for marrying a man whose primary goal was the satisfaction of self, a man devoid of simple common sense. I even blamed Patrick for placing himself in the position where he *could* be arrested, and the suspicions of the police became mine. I traveled to the station, sat and waited at the reception, brought food and fresh water and bags of lemon sherbet, which Patrick loved when he was in court, but I was engaged in a process of divorcing my husband even then, I was mentally severing the ties that bonded me to him and he could feel it from his cell, everyone could, his parents and mine, it was written on my body like a tattoo.

The partners went all out for my husband, I give them that. Every day they would march into the station, brief me on the day's business, how Patrick was holding up, march into his cell. Hours later, sometimes late in the evening, they would be back, then it was debriefing, what they said, what he said, what it all amounted to. They assured me there was no evidence. Many eyewitnesses had stepped up to corroborate my husband's statement:

park-goers, staff at the takeout, people on the street, the operator when he called 999. The partners promised it would go no further; the detectives were reasonable, far from zealous, the partners already in the process of setting him free. When I asked about cost they kissed me on both cheeks, shook their heads, and changed the subject. They did that whenever I mentioned money, and eventually I stopped trying.

Lonely evenings, a full house, myself and the dog in my bedroom, where I'd taken to hiding. A handful of thick hair, huge gleaming scissors. Facing myself in the mirror, squeezing my thumb and first finger together, hearing the *scrunch*, feeling release, relief. Down stairs, cold air on warm skin, unclothed, holding the banister tight in case I fell. Shocked faces. Silence. Jackie and Frank leaving not long afterward, the rot had begun. Father taking me back to my room, Mother's tears.

The detectives were as the partners had described. Casual to the point of distraction, shirts and ties, crumpled jackets. Serious eyes. Always working, wasn't hard to tell. Calm and respectful, constantly called me *madam*. The one that spoke most, said his name was Seth, walked into the reception the first time we met properly, after my husband's arrest, and couldn't take his eyes from me. It was obvious. We'd met before, of course we had, at the house, the press conference, but this was the first time he had seen the real me, not the monster, though I had become some new creature even then, less the woman with the ponytail that fell to my rear, who smiled and danced and posed for cameras, now the one with a shoulder-length bob, who looked at her hands, spoke in a hoarse whisper, eyes dark from lack of sleep. He stammered a lot, something I guessed was unusual, because the other detective kept looking at him. Seth was so sincere, so awkward, I knew I'd made an ally. Even in my desperate state I recognized that he might help, began to do what little I could to make sure he did.

Their apologies, heads bowed, gracious. Patrick emerging from a side door wearing the same clothes, drawn, colorless. I wanted to support him but I didn't have strength. In my mind I did it, reached for him, hugged him, whispered it was okay. In reality there was no recognition, a blank. I was a dying star exploding into supernova, energy dispelled, throwing off my outer shell to reveal a core that shrunk to a tenth of my original size, spinning thirty times a second. I was the black hole that absorbed not light, but emotion, and nothing in my immediate vicinity could escape.

In our home, nothing remained. Mother treated my husband as well as she could, but it was in her eyes. Father hardly spoke. Patrick's parents visited for a few days, and then went back to the States; work matters, they said. Jackie and Frank called, didn't come. Even Caesar was subdued, skulking from us whenever we reached, lowering mournful eyes. Perhaps he wondered where the baby had gone. Seventy days by then, and we were just beginning to face the possibility that our son wasn't coming home.

Seth and Francis came to keep us informed. There were leads, no arrests. That didn't go down well with Patrick, who was attempting to sue the police. Seth would always watch me when he thought no one was looking, but I didn't mind. It would help my cause. My parents left, came back every day, as did others, but we finally had the house to ourselves. People grow tired of grief, especially protracted grief, especially when it concerns the unthinkable, a child. We were living proof that it happened if you weren't vigilant, and we saw stark evidence in each other's eyes. I slept in Malakay's bedroom. Patrick was grateful for that, I always thought. Even hearing him move about the house was too much. I took to wearing earplugs, confining myself, coming out when he'd left. Whole days passed without seeing each other.

It was only a matter of that old foe, time. Quicker than I could tell, I was sitting in the living room eating cornmeal porridge, when I saw a news report. Still no leads in the case of the missing baby, snatched from a locked car nine months ago. And I was spellbound. I hadn't realized. I looked around the wreck of the house, down at the bowl, and saw what everyone had. Patrick had left four months ago, I worked back. Jackie said something about a junior at his firm, ten years younger, looked like I had. I got up, bones aching from sitting prone, sifting through an enormous pile of letters on the kitchen table. Each one was red, demanding. We would have to sell almost everything we owned.

෯

The silence of night is like a cocoon, it makes me feel safe, makes me feel coupled with something larger than myself, yet I am formless and free and able to move in whichever direction I wish, I am both comforting and comforted and knowing nothing does not subtract from my ability to know everything, all it takes is a spoonful of sugar and a little belief and it all comes back to you, so I need not feel fear or anguish, for these are human emotions and at this point I have become more than the sum of my whole, I have become my first my last and my everything, and I have no need to cry, and I need not care about death, and I begin to wonder: is this how the womb felt?

∽

The meninges is the system of membranes which envelope the central nervous system. They consist of three layers: the *dura mater*, the *arachnoid mater*, and the *pia mater*. Their primary function is to protect the brain.

∽

I brought the pecans to Ida, went home. I tidied up, which took less than ten minutes, and made myself lunch. Of course, there was nothing on TV so I switched to the afternoon play on Radio 4, and when that was over, Smooth FM. I mooched around the flat, opened the windows, and inhaled the rich smell of baking, listening to the shouts and loud voices of the block.

Ida knocked as the light began to dim, half a pie beneath a tea towel balanced in one hand. I let her in, made the tea. We played *Blackjack*, or as Ida liked to call it, "Strip Jack Naked." I really liked Ida back then. Our conversations were always languid, gentle debate where neither of us had any particular interest in trumping the other, like our games. There were long pauses while we listened to a news item, or considered our hand, or hummed to a song on the radio. I could always tell the amount of time she was willing to spend in my company by the games she wanted to play. *Blackjack* was a quickie, *Connect 4* a little longer, chess meant I'd better break out the Baileys, *Scrabble* could take all night. We like the same things, Ida and I, old movies, old books, board games and playing cards, cakes and cups of tea. When I'd first moved into the building she would cook me Desperate Dan–sized pies. Her steak and ale was a monster, a joy to consume.

We played three rounds before Ida said she'd better make a start with dinner. I was disappointed, but said it was fine. The wait would be more acute when I was alone, and if I had company when he came, I might consider opening the door. There was another, less subtle motive for wanting Ida to stay, although I was trying not to think about that. As soon as she left it began to nag. I decided to get it over with before I lost my nerve.

I turned down the radio, picked up the phone. Frank answered on the first ring.

—Hello?

—It's me, Frank.

—Who's *me*?

—Don't be an arse, I said, and winced when he dropped the phone. I heard him call Jackie, surprisingly loud for such a mousey man, and a clatter of incomprehensible noise I almost believe she inflicted on purpose.

—Beverley.

—Hello, Jackie. How are you?

—Fine. You?

—Fine.

—What have you been up to?

—Teaching. Ida made pecan pie.

—Yummy.

Not one ounce of enthusiasm.

—I don't want to keep you long, it's just that something strange has happened and I wanted to let you know.

—I see . . .

Straining against curiosity, I could feel it.

—What do you mean by strange?

Frank's voice, distant; he was probably sitting in his favorite chair, the threadbare one, all red with a huge cushion.

—Have you got me on speakerphone?

Jackie considered how best to reply.

—Yes, but—

—Take me off.

—Beverley. Don't start.

—Would you please take me off the speakerphone, Jackie?

Silence, then a click, and the steady hum I hadn't noticed was gone.

—Thank you.

—What do you want to tell me?

—All right, Jackie. Have it your way.

A rumble of quiet obstinacy made the speakers crackle.

—I think I saw Malakay.

Elongated silence. I spoke in a rush, wanting to engulf it.

—Yesterday. He followed me down the street. He came to the flat knocking on the door at two in the morning but I didn't want to let him in because I wasn't sure.

This particular pause was so long I thought she'd hung up.

—Jackie?

—Why would you say that?

—Because it's true. I'm not saying I'm entirely sure, but it's too much of a coincidence to be anything else, and when I looked into his eyes—

—He was a baby.

—Yes, I know that.

—He'd be twenty years old. You can't tell.

—All right. I know it seems hard to explain, but some things in the face—

—Unexplainable, more like. Have you been seeing Sue?

I glared at my possessions, the quiet room.

—Yes, of course. Why would you ask?

—Have you told her?

—Yes. She said I should call the police.

—And stay away from that boy.

—I'll call them, but if he comes again I'll talk to him.

—Yes, well, you'll be sorry.

—Thanks for the confidence, sis. Real supportive.

—Well, you insist on cavorting with those feral children, so what do you expect me to—

I hung up.

Pacing from window to wall, fists balled, cursing between clenched teeth until I caught myself. Stupid. Entirely stupid. I looked from my open window, desperate for some sign, but there was only the recognizable local lot, the kids I'd seen earlier. The sky was dark yet there were bright streaks of red like bleeding fissures, leaking light, illuminating clouds. I closed my eyes until I'd recaptured the calm I felt when Ida was sitting across the table from me. I put on a CD, Joe Harriott, sold to me by the man who worked in the jazz store on Portobello. He told me Harriott and I looked so alike we could have been related. I think it was meant as a compliment.

My night was filled with television, writing, pecan pie, and hot tea. The news was the usual sorrows; I turned over. At midnight I began to nod. I switched to coffee, frothing up warm milk and adding it to my mug, sitting on the sofa in pajamas and a dressing gown, feet snug in furry slippers. Just past one I began to hear strange noises at my door; scratching, bumps, feral as Jackie suggested. The creak of my letter box as it opened slowly and shut, three times, in slow succession.

I curled my knees against my chest, just looking. Why did he come so late? All day I'd been waiting, he could have come anytime. I wasn't going to let him in, no matter how politely he knocked. I pulled my knees in tighter, stomach queasy, lips dry. I smelled sharp coffee on my breath and realized my mouth was wide open.

Another trio of knocks, tentative as the first, my landing light blinking on the doormat. Morse code for *let me in*. I swung my legs, placed my feet in the furry slippers. Slow, ever so slow, trying to be silent. Picked up the oversized wrench I'd found in my old toolbox and placed under a sofa cushion, crept to the front door. If I strained my ears I could hear the faint shift of body weight, the static hiss of clothing, his stuffy nose, blocked, causing him to breathe heavily. The letter box flap drew back, light streamed in, and dust motes spun. I was distracted; they reminded me of my dream. The flap reached a pinnacle, held poised.

—What do you want? I whispered.

He fell back, let go; the flap gave a mute tap. I heard a noise as he hit the metal railings on our landing, it must have been hard because he gasped in pain. Then nothing. I could tell he was there, could just make out rapid snorting. I closed my eyes, raised the wrench.

—I'm not letting you in. Creeping two steps closer. Why do you come so late?

More shuffling. His breathing calmed. The shuffling came nearer.

—Beverley Masters?

That voice. Coarse and deep, more like the kids I taught in the club than the one I imagined for years, the one I heard when I watched him as a baby, asleep in my arms. I squeezed my eyelids shut. I began to see drifting red dots, but the tears still came, rolled down my nose and onto my slippers. My head dropped. I put down the wrench.

—That was my husband's name. I use my maiden name now.

A long, long wait.

—Why?

—It's hard to explain. I can, but not through the door.

—Let me in. We can talk.

—No.

—Why not?

—I don't know who you are.

—Yes you do.

I took a step back, eyed the door.

—You're the boy who followed me from Portobello. That's all.

—No it's not. Why you cryin if I am?

I swiped at my eyes.

—Very clever.

—I'm not tryin to be. I jus wanna come in, talk. It's freezin.

—Well, you can't. You could be anyone, and I don't let anyone in at— I looked at my watch. One thirty-nine in the morning. Do you understand?

—You know who I am.

—I do not.

—Beverley. You *know* who I am.

We listened, unsure.

—Don't say that.

—Why?

—Because I know who you *think* you are. And it's not enough. Not yet.

—Not *enough* . . .

Raised indignation, voice receding, and it was all I could do not to call out. I touched the door, held my palm against wood. I felt cold and became aware of the draft, wept in silence.

—Not yet, I said. I need to know more. I can't let you into my house this late, you must know that . . .

—Proof, the boy said, and I heard louder shuffling.

—What?

—You need proof.

The flap opened. The light was almost celestial; I quieted the thought. I needed vigilance, clarity, not open-hearted weakness. I wiped at my eyes, clenching my jaw in order to make it hurt, to remind myself. I felt pain. There was a noise at the letter box, the boy pushing something through, a folded piece of paper that fell to my doormat, and for one quick moment there was a glimpse of long, stub-ended fingers, eager eyes. I leaned forward to get a better look, but the flap closed, and my slipper was nudging the scrap beneath me.

The paper was folded in half, sideways, a central crease along the middle. I opened it two-handed, like a one-page book. I bit my lip to catch the involuntary whimper. I held the paper toward what little light there was.

A newspaper cut out, dated April 20, 1991. The press conference. Myself, Patrick, Seth, and Francis beside him looking bored. The rest of us in stereotypical freeze-framed grief—Seth, glaring into the camera as if hoping to catch the perpetrator's eye, scare the guilt from him; Patrick looking at the conference table as though the patterns of the tablecloth held meaning; and me, the red-faced monster, paper in one hand, tissue in the other, a seething, bawling mess. I didn't read the article because I knew it by heart. There was a time when I'd owned a full scrapbook of the memories I'd accumulated. Now, the newspaper clippings were the few images of my son that remained; final evidence of a life before. Proof that I had suffered, shed tears, my son had been real.

I moved closer, rough doormat underfoot.

—Are you in pain?

He didn't know what to make of that. The shuffles became pronounced, and the door bounced with the draft.

—How d'you mean?

—When you fell against the railing. Does it hurt?

Surprise. He'd forgotten.

—Why you tryina change subject?

I cringed at his pronunciation, the accent, heard

the tight slap of my dream mother. I shook the scrap of paper.

—This doesn't prove anything.

A moment's consideration.

—Yeah. Yeah, I get you.

—I need more proof.

—I got it. Jus not right now.

—That's fair enough. You can stay or come back in the morning, I don't mind. At first light I'll let you in. Promise.

—All right. Thanks. I think I'll stay.

—Okay. Do you need a blanket?

—Yes, please.

—It'll be thin, but it's better than nothing.

—Thanks, Mum.

I didn't try to correct him. It was good manners for any young man of Caribbean heritage to call a woman older than himself "Mum," or "Auntie," and that was the reason I told myself, no other. I got up, woke my sleeping leg with thumps, and walked into my bedroom, riffled through drawers. I retrieved my own blanket from the sofa and went back, fed the thinner of the two through the letter box. It was slow going, but he was determined and as I felt the cold more acutely since I'd made my decision, I was better for it. Not much, just a little. When the last corner was through, I sat with my back against the wall and pulled my own blanket to my chin. I wouldn't sleep much, but at least I could sit in the dark and know it was our first night together in many years.

❦

When speaking about pain, the poet Emily Dickinson wrote, *"It has no future but itself."*

～

I am a smooth, rounded pebble in the snow. I am featureless rock, a white cliff. I am a mannequin, a human facsimile. I am void.

Conversely, even as I think this, I become aware of the pulse at my fingertips, the dance of floaters before my eyes, and the tickle of irritation that forms an itch. I am conscious of the fact that I recently forgot to cut my nails and my big toe sometimes catches on my tights. I can hear the tick of the central heating, that miniature drumbeat, and the creaks of my flat, like a tired body that has found rest. I take note of the saliva that glides down my throat when I swallow, the slim remnants of dinner in my teeth. It's a luxury to feel these things without physical pain, without injury, able of body and arguably mind. I hereby resolve to make the most of my time, to harbor experience like a miser hoards riches, close to his chest, gloating over every note.

～

How much is that doggie in the window?

～

Morning light. Sharp, almost piercing. Tapping my eyelids. I stretched, remembered, looking at the blank sheen of my door, rolling my neck, savoring cracks. When I pushed myself to my feet with one hand, pain shot through me. I thought of him on my landing, told myself to ignore what I felt, it was nothing in comparison.

I brewed tea, broke eggs, whipped and poured them into the frying pan, made toast. The digital clock on my stove said six. I put everything on a tray and carried it to the door. Tray on one side, front door open, I looked at the boy. There wasn't much to see, but that didn't matter.

He was hunched, trembling. It seemed the landing amplified the wind, collecting it at one end and rushing it down the other, ice cold, northerly, the experts would have said. He was asleep, a flimsy sliver of shut-eye. Thick jacket, hood covering his head, scarf across his mouth. Thick gloves made for motorcycles; at least he'd been prepared.

I laid a hand on his shoulder, shook. Searched his eyes for some recognition when they opened, his or mine, and though I would have liked to see what I told Jackie I had noticed from yards away, the stab in my gut was enough; if it was him, there was no trace. Everything I knew was scrubbed away and remade, millions of cells engaged in constant death and rebirth how many times over? Well, if the human body regenerates every seven years, that would mean this was the end of his third incarnation, and the first, the one I had known, was dancing in some spiritual ether, if such a thing existed, though I was aware my thoughts were based on hope rather than belief. He didn't recognize me either, even though his sad eyes crinkled like he was smiling. I turned away, unable to hold them, trying to see if anyone noticed us, and wondered what was going on.

He got to his feet, wincing. He was huge, like his long-dead grandfather, like everyone on our side. I backed into the flat and he followed. How dark it was, how strange it must have seemed, to be led into an unfamiliar flat by an unfamiliar woman. Mum. Such a comfy, cozy word.

Blanket held close, shutting the door behind him, he stood in the passage. I beckoned him further. He unclipped the chinstraps of his hood, revealed his face. Nothing. No sensation, familiarity. We searched each other's features.

—I made breakfast. Eggs and toast.

—Thanks . . . Mum.

He mumbled the single word. Even he wasn't sure, now that I stood before him, tall and real. I flinched.

—You'd better get some tea inside you, warm up.

He sat at my coffee table, gazing at the tray. I wondered if he liked eggs until I realized his lips were moving. Prayers. I couldn't hear if they were Christian or Islamic, or something else, the solitary words mumbled into his chest as though he was confiding in his heart, and then he was grasping the knife and fork like reins, and his head was bowing, and he was cutting, lifting, and eating. And the strangest feeling came over me. It's difficult to explain. I grew warm, almost light-headed, and I sat on the arm of my sofa, something I never do, watching him almost force feed himself, or at least that's what it looked like. The smile was fighting for possession of my lips, and so I ducked my head. It was on the verge of terrifying, this euphoria that swept my body, making me jitter with unreleased energy. I breathed in through my nose and out through my mouth, though it was tough because I was grinning.

He was watching. It must have seemed as though I was going to be sick, hands on my knees, head between my legs, huffing air.

—You all right?

—Yes, yes, I'm fine. Eat.

—I'm finished.

—Do you want more?

—No thanks.

He sat back, eyes running over everything.

—Would you like to sleep? I could make up the sofa bed and go shopping. Then we could talk.

—Thank you.

I took his tray and set up the sofa bed. It wasn't the most comfortable, but after the landing it must have seemed like luxury. He tried to help, but we were awkward and I preferred to do it myself. It felt like a blind date, although that confused me even more and I didn't like the connotations. He stood to one side, looming, hands by his thighs. I plumped up pillows and spent time tucking in sheets, pulling down duvet corners so I wouldn't have to look. Then I took a shower, which allowed him time to undress and get into bed.

I did not wash in the true sense of the word. I wanted to, but the water sent me deeper into my own mind, my trance if you will. I was still smiling, and the thoughts were coming, flashes of past and recent events, my maddening attempts to photo-fit the face in my living room with the face I had known, the niggling wriggle of mistake, the thought I could be wrong. My awareness that even those suspicions could lead me astray. And the water beat down on my head and all I could hear was thunder, and all I could see was the past, present, and all of my possible futures raining down, each a tiny droplet, a cascade of everything that was and could be. And I immersed myself in it, I would like to say I cried and I even pretended I did when the water got into my eyes, but that was a lie, there was nothing, only my thoughts and the needle sensation of hot water. I let it burn until my skin was raw.

∽

The one with the waggly tail?

∽

Years since I had been in love, and yet I remembered the glow. The saturated color it gives the world, the way sounds become more acute. An insect buzzes past your head, too quick to be seen, but there's the feeling of almost making contact, of knowing you are part of a bigger world. Starts you thinking: are we just a fading buzz in a larger ear? Look to the sky and try to imagine something that big, only to be caught by the fingernail curve of the moon. See beauty again, up there, even down amongst dirty sidewalks, shouted commerce, exhaust fumes, and the loud voice of engines. Nod hello at people you know, see them wonder what makes you so cheerful this morning, frown, good mood is unwelcome in the land of gloom. Too many gray days, too much rain to recognize when spring has truly arrived, but the feeling of love saturated me, unwillingly perhaps, guiding my steps. I even hummed a Harriott melody as I scoured shelves and tried to remember what men liked to eat.

❧

Arachnoiditis is a condition in which the *arachnoid mater* becomes inflamed. A number of causes, including infection or trauma, can result in the inflammation. Arachnoiditis can be known to produce disabling, progressive, and even permanent pain.

❧

Him on the extended sofa bed, me on the opposite easy chair. Nervous, both of us, now the time had come. Tiny specks of dampness between my fingertips. Sparks of excitement. Unable to hold his eye, speaking in a low mumble. Him clutching a mug of tea, shielding his face. Sniffling and wiping his nose with his hand. The huge jacket removed, a plain and thin faded T-shirt that sagged at the neck, gray tracksuit bottoms. Hair uncombed, uncut, peaked like a cockerel's comb. He wore gray socks, but with his feet outstretched I could see translucent soles. I didn't want to notice how black they were, wonder how many times they'd been worn.

When I came back from the supermarket, he was asleep. Even when I kicked the front door shut and took the shopping into the kitchen, he didn't wake up. Something in the air smelled wrong. I stood straight. I unpacked and went into the living room, wanting to look without shame. He was skinny. There were dark marks on his arms, various cuts and bruises and I leaned closer, but it was difficult to tell whether they'd been caused by genuine accidents or something he had done. His peach fuzz was a wisped tangle of matted hair and shaving bumps. His skin was overcast with grime, and now that I was closer it was clear the wrong smell came from him, was him, it rolled off his body in waves, a musky odor of man I had long forgotten.

I went away, made tea, and came back to the boy. I rocked his arm until he stirred.

—Well, I said. I don't know which of us should start.

He sipped tea. I noted lengthy, dark fingernails.

—I mean, where to begin? This is all so strange.

—Tell me about yourself, he said. What do you do?

—I teach, I told him. I'm a teacher. Not officially, for a school, but I run an after-school club . . .

—At the youth center?

—That's right.

—But you was a teacher before, yeah?

—I was. I've given that up, a long time ago.

He nodded, somber.

—What else?

I tried to think of something. I really did. I looked into a corner of the room and wracked my brain. But there was nothing. That was the last twenty years. I taught. When I tried to examine what else I might have thought and done, there was nothing, and that came as a shock. I gripped my mug.

—That's it, really. Nothing else.

He was nodding again, that made sense. Maybe thinking I could have done more with my time, looked for him. The After-School Club seemed like an indulgence when faced with his tired eyes and defeated slump.

—What about you? Why do you always come at night, don't you have anywhere to stay?

—Yeah, he said. I got somewhere.

—Where? With friends, a girlfriend . . . ?

—A girl who's a friend. From school. She lets me sleep in her flat while her man's at work, but when he comes home I gotta leave. She lives in Earl's Court. I've been there awhile, but it's not workin out.

—Why?

Alert, mug warming my knees.

—He don't like me . . . She tries to tell him we're friends but he don't believe her.

—And where do you stay when he comes back?

He shrugged.

—Other friends' floors. The park. It's not so cold.

—How long have you been doing that?

—Not long. Awhile.

He lowered his head until all I could see was matted hair. I crossed the room, sat close. Put my hand on his.

—You can stay as long as you like. In the meantime we can find the proof. There's a policeman—

He looked up. I jumped, lifting my hand.

—I don't wanna talk to no police.

Tone firm, chin raised.

—We must . . .

—I don't wanna. Promise.

He wouldn't meet my eye. I put my hand back.

—Okay . . . That's fine . . .

Tension, even in his knuckles. Rigid tendons, fingers curled as if for cover, an almost fist. A tattoo high on his bicep. Blue ink, simple lettering. *Eddie.*

—Sorry if I scared you.

—That's all right, I said. So, do you . . . Can you tell me anything about what happened? After the . . . When you were taken? I forced myself to smile. As you can imagine, I've been desperate.

—Yeah.

I bowed my head until it was level with his.

—Could you tell me? Please?

—Yeah.

He sat with both hands around the mug. I thought it would be better if I didn't push, so I rubbed those bony knuckles and gave him time. He seemed to be thinking. About the past, if he could trust me enough, whether he could invent some tall tale, I couldn't tell. We sat for a long time, nothing said, him cradling the mug like an artifact.

—He was a man, he said, at last.

—Who took you? He was male?

—Yeah, he said. He was old back then. I thought.

—Was he black, white, Asian?

I could feel the old panic, a jumbling of words that bounced and knocked against my throat, and when I wrenched myself away from the images in my head the boy was staring at me. I gulped, took a thin sip of cold tea. Pursed my lips and pushed my knees together.

—He was black, the boy said into his mug. I suppose that's how he got away with it.

—I suppose.

—First there were three of us. He had a wife. We lived lotsa places. Shepherd's Bush, Edward Woods, Olympia . . . Then she passed. Rosie died an he went funny. Didn't talk much. Left me to myself.

—Did they look after you? You know . . . like parents? Or . . .

He turned from me. I started to cry. His back was broad, so skinny I could see the triangular peaks of his shoulder blades through the unwashed T-shirt.

—They tried. One day at a time, he said. He had problems but he was workin on them.

—What was his name? The old man?

—Eddie. He was tryin, honestly.

—I'm sure he was. Did you attend school?

—Rosie took care of that. Said I was her sister's kid, said she passed away.

—Where did you go?

—A few places.

I wiped my eyes, trying to focus.

—Why a few?

He was silent for more than five minutes, shivering every so often. He muttered under his breath, shards of half sentences. I went cold. Watched him converse with himself. I cried more, though it could hardly have been called that. The tears just came, one at a time, halting, reluctant to leave.

—Why a few, Malakay?

He gave me a sorrowful look.

—I got kicked out. Sent to a unit.

My body contracted. He could perceive it, I saw, probably guessed my reaction before it came.

—Would you like lunch?

He nodded. I went into the kitchen and wiped my eyes with a tea towel, started to prepare. He came, stood by the door. I didn't want to face him. Jackie always said I had expressive eyes, and it's true. Emotion runs over them like patterns on seashells. I am most vulnerable when they are heightened, and I couldn't possibly let him see that. My doubt, my suspicion, my fear.

He waited. Every now and then he would sniff, and I wanted to tell him to blow his nose. I was grateful he didn't come closer, as he'd brought the odor with him. Not exactly unpleasant, not cologne. I found myself wondering if he could smell me. The stench of disappointment churned with sorrow. *Eau de Bev.*

—There's proof at the house.

A thin square of sliced ham drooped between my fingers. He looked scared.

—Sorry?

—If you want proof, Eddie's got it. That's how I found out, innit? I saw the proof, that's why I left. He wasn't happy.

—I see.

I laid ham onto bread, bread onto ham; shook a box of paper-wrapped prawns onto a baking tray, slid them into the oven.

—Here's the keys. I'll give you the address if you want. You can talk to him yourself.

I smarted despite myself, stung by his casual air, the ludicrous suggestion, the singing jangle of unseen keys.

—So what am I supposed to do, pop over and say hello? Bake him a cake, make a house call?

I put the remaining prawns back in the freezer. The boy sighed.

—I'll come. We'll go together. He's sorry, he said that. He'll tell you everything. He's in a better place.

A rattle of metal against metal, the thump. I closed my eyes. Forced myself to speak calmly.

—Lunch will be ready in twenty minutes. Would you like to wash up?

—Yes, please.

Worried, hoping he hadn't done something wrong.

—Go to the bathroom. I'll get you a towel. Be there in a minute.

He left. I heard the bathroom door close and allowed myself to crumple. I wept against the kitchen counter, mouth closed, one arm over my head.

≺৹

How much is that doggie in the window?

≺৹

A few days before the house was sold, I had a sudden panic attack. I'd moved into the Ladbroke Grove flat a week before, and was still engaged in transition. There were boxes everywhere. I was waiting for a new bed to be delivered and I was using the sofa bed until it arrived. Clothes were in black plastic bags. My personal effects were scattered on work surfaces and tables. Caesar was equally unsettled; he walked from room to room sniffing boxes, whining.

I was looking for a novel I'd misplaced when I came across the contract of sale for my old home. I read the details, even though I'd gone over them repeatedly with my lawyer, with Seth, and, for the little time I could stand, with Patrick and the new owners. The black lines blurred and I was seeing the night I brought Malakay home wrapped in a white cotton blanket. The creak of the opening door, waiting by the stairs. Patrick moving ahead to switch on lights. Me lifting the baby to my nose, burying my head in thin hair. Patrick laughed whenever he saw me, said, "She's smelling the baby again." That night he was meters in front of me, and in those scant moments it was only me and Malakay, the darkness, only for a few seconds at most, but we were together and I breathed in all I could gather and there was nothing to be seen, every sensation was us.

When I came to I was screaming. Stumbling over boxes, lashing air, Caesar jumping and yelping by my side. I couldn't breathe. I gasped, clawed my throat. I thought I was going to die. I fumbled to the front door, tripped, fell. Caesar was licking my face and I think that's what saved me, the fact that I hate being licked by animals, especially on my face, and the horror broke my panic. I sucked in a huge breath and when it came out, all the tension went. I coughed and stroked the dog, forced myself to respire in a drawn-out fashion. I sat up, gasping, in shock.

That settled it, for me. I had to do something. I snatched keys from a table, got into my car. I was driving a forlorn Mini Cooper then.

The parking lot outside the Chinese takeout was vacant. I slipped the car into the space I imagined Patrick had claimed, stopped. Got out, paced up and down. Pedestrians tried not to look. I was angry. I'd thought I'd feel something—some trace, some vibration—but my body was numb.

When I pulled up on my former road I sat awhile. The house was impartial. It had no sympathy for me, or Patrick. I was disappointed. I'd expected solidarity, loose tiles, broken windows. Dilapidated sorrow for lives moved on. Seen from my dirty car windows, the house looked like a whore. Painted, alluring, open to all.

I slammed my Mini door, crossed the road with the old keys swinging on a finger. No exchange, possession was nine-tenths. It was gray and dark that day, perfect cover. I let myself in easily, as if I had business.

Empty rooms. The echo of my heels, clipped and satisfying. Swept and polished, I could smell it. I went into the kitchen. Someone had left a small kettle, a box of tea bags, and a duo of washed mugs. The fridge was empty, switched off, so I had mine black. I walked into the living room. Everything was gone, even then, all those happy moments. I only remembered the random flicker of television, us holding each other's hands and not feeling, each unaware of the other, cordless between us like a small pet. I strained. Really. Furrowed my brow and tried and saw the time Patrick came home early with wine, brown stew chicken in aluminium containers, a couple of VHS tapes from the local store, and we didn't even get past the first, or finish the meal, because we ended up making love on the floor, right where I was looking, going up to the bedroom and doing it again, and again.

I held the mug against my breast, smiled. There had been a before. I remembered. I walked with considered steps, deciding if what I saw was suitable. Imagining household items in empty spaces, reinhabiting rooms as if they were mine. Prospecting for memories. Upstairs, I avoided the closed door and went to the master bedroom. The broad panorama of central windows, houses opposite, brown, yellow, pink. Pale floorboards, white walls, bare bed. I lay on the mattress holding my tea, let my legs hang from the foot of the bed, and remembered

that night, many others. There had been a before. There
had.

The bathroom. Jostling each other, toothbrush in
mouths, muttered chatter between projectile spitting.
The spa bath. Champagne on the night we moved in,
had forgotten that. The study. Patrick on his dark-screen
PC, surrounded by open books, red eyes, ballpoint between fingers. Me saying, *Knock knock*. Cocoa and kisses,
easing onto his lap. The landing, baby crawling from the
nursery toward the stairs, grasping the gate like a pris-
oner, hauling himself up and smiling at whoever greeted
him. Cries splitting the night. Creeping from the bedroom with half-closed eyes, one hand on my dressing
gown, the other feeling its way toward the baby's new
territory, a whole world to him. One hand outstretched,
stumbling, palm against wood, to push my way into . . .

The nursery. How small, how empty. That smell of
him, all gone. Only wood polish, disinfectant, fresh air
from open windows. I felt annoyed with myself, because I should have said something. I should have told
them the room was to be left until the very last minute. I
should have known I would crave the odor I was trying
to recall, straining to recapture, and it's amazing how
such things are gone forever, that you can recollect how
things looked and sounded, even how things tasted and
felt, but you try to remember a smell, go on, I challenge
you now, try and bring back a scent from the past so you
can smell it anew and you will be beaten, I can assure
you, it's just not possible, unless you are lucky enough
to come across the odor again, in which case it can be
like hearing a piece of music, it all comes flooding back.

I waited, knowing it wouldn't happen, hoping, nose

raised, trying to catch something. A car pulled up on the street, the engine died. Something told me to go and look, see if the estate agent was back. He wasn't. It was Patrick.

He stepped from the Saab 9000, his pride and joy, the car our child was stolen from. Looked up and down the street, rearranged his suit. He crossed the road and came up the garden path as if he'd never left.

The door slammed. I left the nursery, walked halfway down. He heard my heels, hesitated. Listened, I could feel it. Turned and walked to the foot of the stairs, placed a gleaming brown shoe on the first step. He did that whenever I was in the bedroom and he was downstairs, whenever he wanted to speak with me.

"Hello?"

"Hello, Patrick."

"Beverley? What the hell?"

I came down the stairs. My first thought was: how handsome. A light smell of Polo cologne. The suit, Yves Saint Laurent. The shirt, Gucci. I'd bought them. The purple went well with gray.

"I could say the same thing. This is a little unexpected. And awkward."

"Couldn't get enough of the old place, could we? Lots of memories."

Hand on the banister, smiling.

"Some better than others," I said, going down the stairs, into the kitchen. "Some I'd rather not remember."

I washed the mug and shook the water off, and when I turned he was biting his lip, testing the living room floorboards with a foot.

"Good job repointing, don't you think?"

I slammed the mug against the counter. It smashed, left me with the handle. Bone china everywhere, shards skittering into the sink. Fingers humming. My ears shrieked.

"Damn it, Beverley! Are you crazy?"

I brandished the handle at him.

"Why? Are you?"

"You're being totally unreasonable."

"No I'm not, and you know it."

I threw the handle into the sink, started to walk past Patrick. He grabbed me.

"You wait a minute—"

"Get your fucking hands off me!" Patrick recoiled, shocked into letting go. I pushed again, bumped against him. His body, still firm. "Move!"

"Beverley . . ."

"I said move!"

"Will you just shut the hell up?"

I didn't see it. Just felt sharp pain across my face and my legs were weak, feet removed beneath me, and I was falling, flailing against air until my back hit the counter, and I gasped, arched, crumpled. Patrick was beside me, reaching for my shoulders again.

"Beverley!" he cried. "Beverley!"

"Leave me alone!"

I was screaming, beating his hands. He tried to help me up.

"Beverley, I don't know what happened—"

I roared, pushed him away, mouth open, a harsh, throaty cry. Patrick backed off when he heard it, fist in mouth, pacing the tiled floor. Blubbering like a two-year-old.

"I don't understand," he whispered. "I don't. I'm

suffering too, you know? You think I don't feel regret? Don't think about it? He was my son too. He was my flesh and blood and I know I was there, but we all lose focus. We all lapse. I'm human, Beverley, what the hell do you expect? Perfection? Well, I'm sorry, we can't all be you, we can't all meet your expectations, all I was trying to do was make an attempt, you know, you were always hungry and upset there was no food, and I wanted to have something ready when you came home, for you, and I should have gone shopping, but I was *tired*, Beverley. I was up all night but I doubt if you remember, you were wrapped up with Malakay, the job, your fucking *career*, and you didn't think about me, so I got hungry, and I got tired, and I lost focus, and it was only five minutes there and back, five minutes, and now you hate me, I hate myself, everyone hates me."

An explosion of tears he attempted to stem with his fist. I wanted to feel pity, but I was trying to bring another scent back from the past. I got to my feet, woozy, wary. Right cheek burning.

"Goodbye, Patrick."

I walked out with dignity. I heard movement behind me and forced myself not to look, or run.

"I see him!" Patrick screamed. "I see him every night, does that satisfy you?"

Outside, it was quiet. One of the things we'd loved about our street. I closed the door, looked both ways, crossed. I started the Mini and left. I suppose I've been leaving ever since.

❦

I do hope that doggie's for sale.

❧

While he was in the shower, I went into the bedroom and dug in my filing cabinet. At the bottom of the drawer, beneath the crap I'd collected, I found it. Battered leather, royal blue. Once, it even had the year in gold, although that was long gone, scratched away so all that remained was the ghost of numbers. Fitting. I flicked through soft, darkened pages until I found it. I sat on the bed with my cordless, kept an eye on my open door. I dialed the international code, his number. Heart beating steadily. Throat dry. I kept swallowing, even when I didn't need to.

A bright, friendly voice. Female. Young and efficient. Not here right now, but your call is important. Leave your name and number. Tone.

—Hi, Patrick. This is Beverley. I was wondering if you could give me a call. It's quite important. I'll explain when I hear from you. Love to the family. Be well.

I hung up. In the bathroom, silence. I strained to hear more, could not.

❧

Black boys in secondary school education are three times more likely to face expulsion than their white counterparts. Only fifteen percent of those thrown out are reinstated. Upon leaving primary school, the boys' performance "begins high," but starts to decline by Key Stage 2, tails off by Key Stage 3, and by Key Stage 4 they have fallen behind. Issues of race, class, and gender are cited as primary causes.

❦

I heard him move about the flat, didn't get up. I think I needed time to adjust to his presence. The noises stopped and there was quiet, for a long time. I went into the living room. He sat on the untidily folded sofa. He was staring into space, muttering.

—Feeling better?

He nodded, still and curious.

—I was thinking we should go and get your things. If you have any.

—Yeah . . . okay . . .

He stretched and reminded me of a large dark spider, thick body, protruding limbs.

—Do you need to use the phone? See if she'll be in?

—She'll be in, he said.

On the landing I locked up, the boy beside me. Ida was sweeping her doorstep. When she glanced up she jumped, caught herself, tried to pretend she hadn't.

—Morning.

—Uh . . . Mornin . . .

She stared, realized. I glanced over my shoulder. He'd hardly noticed, or so it seemed.

—This is a friend, a student. He'll be staying awhile.

—Oh. All right then.

—This is Ida.

He nodded, pushing his lips together in that almost smile. I didn't want to say his name for a variety of reasons: I wasn't really sure if it *was* his name; I didn't want Ida to know too much until I knew more; there was no telling how he might react if I kept referring to him by the name I remembered. It struck me for the first time that he must have been called something else all those years, but to ask what seemed insensitive, like every other question I'd harbored and was now afraid to pose. It confused me, and in my confusion I must have acted quite strange, because Ida was giving me a disapproving look. It was very awkward. I walked away quick, out the heavy door and across the road to the Honda. The streets seemed quiet, even though I could hear the midmorning rumble of people, the birds singing as though it was just another day.

It wasn't far to Earl's Court. When I reached Talgarth Road, he directed. A thin street off the main road, cars parked on both sides so we had to drive around the block just to get a space, even though I had a borough-wide permit. I kept watching to see if he was at all fazed by what we were doing, but he seemed in a dream, not talking, spying on the world. Stick-thin cyclists, tourists clutching A-Z guidebooks, women pushing Maclarens and Bugaboos. I asked mundane questions: if he could drive, if he liked living in that part of the city, if he was hungry. He eyed me, seemingly amused. No, yes, a little bit. I felt dreamy too, sensations submerged beneath a dull fog of unknown substance, thick and murky, clouding my view. I locked up and followed him the way we had come, trying to guess what lay before me from my surroundings, a pointless task, but something that kept my mind from the absurdity of our situation.

We turned into a gate, a basement. There were at

least ten flowerpots there, all sizes and colors. The plants looked watered and well fed. Broken kids' toys, a discarded TV and metal stand. An old, cream-colored PC monitor. Lamps, cardboard boxes, more Western waste. He rang the bell. Of course, no one was there. I had my phone, which I gave him. The number was eventually fished out of a floppy Oyster wallet. When she answered, there seemed to be an argument. He took it in his stride, speaking in a calm, neutral tone, but I could hear her shouts from where I was standing. He hung up, handed me the phone, said she would be ten minutes. It was actually closer to half an hour, us sitting on the steps with sore backsides, cold despite the meager sun, and when she turned up pushing a baby stroller laden with plastic shopping bags she gave him such a dirty look I wanted to slap her, or at least say something, and then she noticed me and I could see she was sorry I had seen that, and she mumbled hello at her Nikes.

She didn't seem surprised to see me. That told me something. We helped her bring the stroller down the stairs, cooing at the baby, which I guessed was a girl because the hood and the stroller itself were pink. While we waited for her to unlock the door I thought someone would speak. We didn't even look at each other. The only conversation was between the boy and her daughter, who giggled as he played with her, grasping his finger.

The flat was nice, homely; new beginnings, I guessed from the unmatched furniture, still making adjustments. Kids' toys and photos of the baby. The boyfriend captured in framed doting portraits, soft eyes and clear intent. The boy stood in the center of the living room while his friend went into a bedroom saying she was going to change the baby. We ignored each other. I was feeling more estranged by the second, twirling from item to item, trying not to look. When she came back, baby in arms, we were still standing.

—Take a seat, make yourself at home, she said. I'm Vicky and this is Rae. She held the baby up. Wills is crap at introductions.

—Is he? I said, turning his way. He seemed embarrassed; I guessed it was the name. Me too.

—That's something you have in common, Vicky said. Would you like a drink? Tea, coffee, juice?

—I'll have a tea, thanks. Milk, no sugar.

—What about you?

—Nah, I'm cool. Want me to hold her?

—Yeah, all right.

She passed Rae over and went into the kitchen. The baby seemed to like him. She wrapped an arm around one shoulder and lay against the other, thumb in mouth, eyes open. I crouched beside her and she didn't flinch, just regarded me as though she'd seen my type come and go. Her hair was black cotton candy and her eyes were wide, heavily lashed.

—She's very pretty.

—Yeah. Gonna be a model.

His pride made me smile. I glanced from one face to the other. She didn't look like him. She had the mouth and nose of the man in the pictures.

—You're going to miss her, aren't you?

—Bad, he said. I used to take her to the park . . .

—You still can, you know. I don't mind, and you'd

probably be doing Vicky a favor. Give her time to herself. We could do it together.

—Yeah, he said. His smile was full, the brightest. That'd be cool.

—Hello, Sunray, I said. That's what you are, a little sunray, aren't you?

I stroked her hair. The little girl showed me gums. The throaty voice of the kettle grew loud, clicked into silence. I waited and when I didn't hear anything, I got up.

—Just going to see if Vicky needs help.

He didn't answer, so I left. Vicky had her back against the kitchen counter and was looking at the ceiling. Her fist was covered by her sleeve, pushed into her mouth, and she was shaking. When I came in she turned to face the kitchen wall. I went over and put my arm around her shoulder. She relaxed against me and the shudders got worse, reached a climax, subsided.

—Okay, I whispered. It'll be okay.

—It's not what you think.

—I don't think anything.

—Daryl does. We were close way before him, he don't understand.

I let her go, took mugs off hooks. Reached for the tea container.

—You only have to look at the pictures to see how he feels about you and Rae. He seems like a good man.

—He is, Vicky said. He works really hard.

—He's trying to keep the good things in his life.

—Yeah, but I love him.

—That's obvious.

—No, you don't get me. I love *him*. And Daryl. That's not right, is it?

I watched her sniffle, reach for the roll of kitchen towels. Maybe she was telling the truth.

—Who am I to say? It's complicated, I'll tell you that much. Sugar?

—Yes, please. One an a half.

—A half?

—I'm watchin my weight, she said, and we both laughed. I stirred as Vicky wiped her nose, waited for her to finish. Gave her the mug.

—How long has Wills been here?

—On and off, three or four months. Him and his dad . . . Oh, sorry . . . She reddened. They weren't getting on.

—He was living there? Before?

—Nah, he was in a hostel. But he had to leave.

—Oh.

—I shouldn't say anything . . .

—No, course not. I'll talk to Wills.

We sipped, studied shelves. Vicky realized she was still holding the balled-up tissue and threw it in the trash. Another clang. I winced.

—We knew you'd come. Daryl didn't think you'd believe him, but we knew you'd come. You had to.

—How did you find out? About me, I mean.

—You taught Maxine Yorke, right?

—Yes. Awhile ago. Nice girl.

—She's my half-sister.

—Oh. I can see the resemblance now that you say it.

—Maxi told me what happened. When Wills started goin on about what he found in Eddie's, it made sense. I told him.

—Oh, I said. Well, thank you.

She gave me a tiny, Wills-style smile.

—He's a nice guy. He'll get over it, everyone's got issues.

—Certainly have, I said.

In the living room, Wills was on the floor and Rae was playing with dolls, sitting them before a small table, making them drink empty plastic cups of tea. Wills held a skinny brown one, pretended to make it speak. When he put it down, Rae made him pick it back up and said, Drink.

—Rae, leave him alone, will you?

—He's drinking.

—I am, Wills said. He seemed serious.

—Yeah, well, he hasn't got time for all that. He's got things to do.

—Not until we finish our tea, I said.

Vicky shot me a glance and smiled, did her best to hide it. I crouched down next to Rae, picked up a doll.

❧

Maxine Yorke was a huge girl who towered over her primary school teachers and had the body of an adult, even then. She'd been brainy but loud and her peer group consisted of the sons, daughters, and siblings of criminals. She'd left school with adequate grades, attended the club mostly because her friends did. Although she was polite and well-mannered, she was also hardheaded, easily influenced. We clashed on many occasions. She was always sorry and I became convinced she had the potential to turn things around. When she grew too old for the club, I would sometimes see her clearly intoxicated, in the company of people who were open about who

they were and what they did. Her clothes and hair began to worsen, and she would wander blindly in broad
daylight. One winter I saw her on a sodium-lit corner
and knew the worst had happened. Rumor said Maxine
was admitted to the St Charles' Centre for Health and
Wellbeing. I haven't seen her since.

~§

The *dura mater*, also known as the *meninx fibrosa*, derives
its name from the Latin *dura*, meaning tough, and *mater*,
meaning mother. One of its functions is to carry blood
from the brain to the heart.

~§

On the way home, Wills remained silent. It was close to
rush hour and the traffic was getting heavy. I switched
on the radio, which was tuned to a community station.
They were playing old-time reggae, so I left it.

—She cares about you a lot, you know.

—Yeah . . . Nodding to the music. Yeah, we go way
back.

—Vicky said that. School, right?

—Yeah. We've been good friends.

—She called you Wills. You didn't tell me that was
your name.

He stopped nodding.

—Is that what they called you? Ed and Rosie?

—Nah.

—So which do you prefer? You can be honest, I don't
mind.

He was thinking. I could tell from the tilt of his chin.

—Call me Michael.

—Is that what they called you?

He shook his head.

—I like the way it sounds.

Music filled silence. A motorcycle roared, close on my side.

—Wills is cool though. Just call me Wills, innit.

—But which do you feel like? I don't mind, really. I'll call you what you want.

—I don't feel like nuttin, he said, facing me. I don't feel like nuttin at all.

—Okay, I said. Okay.

The light turned green. Nothing moved.

∽

Dolorimetry (*dolor*: Latin: pain, grief) is the measurement of pain response in animals, including humans.

∽

We got back as the sun went down. Wills hauled his only belongings, a battered tote bag, into the living room and pushed it next to the sofa. I fixed a quick pasta dinner and we ate with plates on knees, watching TV. We were just finished when someone knocked.

—That'll be Ida, I told him. It was.

—Hi, love, she said. Thought you might like a Bakewell tart.

I could smell it beneath the kitchen towel, warm and sweet.

—I'd love it, and I'm sure Wills could eat.

She followed me into the living room where he sat up, alert.

—Hello, love.

—Hello.

He seemed uneasy, mute.

—Ida brought homemade Bakewell tart. Would you like a slice?

—Yes, please.

I steered her toward the kitchen when it became apparent she wouldn't be going by herself. She slid the tart onto my counter, unveiled it. A glorious smell rose, almonds and brown sugar and jam.

—It looks amazing.

—Thanks, thought you'd like it. How many slices?

—Three, but I'll do it. You sit down, you. Probably been on your feet all day. Like a drink?

—A bit of sherry if you have it.

—I most certainly do.

I poured Ida a small glass. I could feel her eyes on me, could hear her brain ticking.

—Seems a nice lad.

It was a lie, although I couldn't think how I would say that without seeming rude. I wanted to tell her the truth, but Ida was a gossip, she couldn't help herself, and it was difficult to fathom what would be worse— her knowing and telling everyone, or her making something up and telling everyone. I wanted to trust Ida, couldn't. I busied myself finding the big knife, going to work.

—He'll be with me until he finds somewhere else. That might be awhile. He's been evicted.

—Oh, right. Seems very nice. Quiet sort.

—Won't get much out of him, that's true. Not like us. Talk the doors off a barnyard, we would.

—If we had anyone else to talk to besides each other, Ida said.

I put the slices onto plates, found cream in my fridge, and poured it into a tiny jug. I moved everything onto a tray.

—That's true, I said. Never mind.

—Well, you do now.

—Yes.

—Nice lad.

—Shall we go through? I said, motioning with my head. You grab the bottle, I'm sure you're not finished yet.

Ida went first. The living room was too dark to see anything. I put down the tray, switched on the lights. Wills jumped as though we'd sneaked up on him, which made Ida lurch in turn. She backed into me, and I bumped the tray. Cream spilled.

—Oh, sorry, love.

—That's okay, it's nothing. I'll go and get some kitchen towels.

I left the room and came back briskly, not wanting to leave them alone. Someone was bound to say the wrong thing; I just couldn't predict who. When I returned they were sitting far apart, Ida's hands on her knees, watching him like television. He was obviously uncomfortable. I cleaned up quickly and sat between them, hoping to break her gaze. The thin, diminutive old woman had turned Wills into a nervous boy in less than five minutes. I was impressed.

—So, what have you been up to? Anything exciting? Front-page news, any raves?

—She's a daft one, Ida said to Wills, who blinked at her. Nope, all quiet. Graham said he'll come down, providing he can get time off.

—Oh, that's good. It's been awhile, hasn't it?

—A few weeks, yes. But he's ever so busy, especially now that things are harder. Funding cuts, you see . . .

—They were threatening that, weren't they?

—Some of the money was private, but most came from the local council and that's all gone. They've had to start a campaign.

—Oh, Ida.

—And if that doesn't work, they might have to shut the whole thing down, if some rich bloke don't come along, or they can't raise money.

—Ida's son and daughter-in-law run a nature retreat, I told Wills. It's quite famous. Lots of celebrity patrons, it's been going for ten years, absolutely gorgeous. It's in Cornwall.

—Ah, said Wills.

—You can see wildlife there, birds mostly, but there are deer, foxes, and the odd badger. And there's a monkey sanctuary nearby.

—Cheeky monkeys, Ida said. One of them nicked my hat years ago. Took it to the top of his tree, shat in it, threw it back down.

Wills joined in with our laughter.

—You didn't tell me that.

—Never went again, mark my words. I was livid.

—Terrible, I said. We'll go there one day, Wills, if you like.

He smiled, nodding. When I turned to Ida her eyes were narrowed and she wasn't laughing anymore. She caught me looking, straightened up.

—Shall we have some of that cake before it goes stone cold?

—Yes, I said, handing out plates. Mine's the small slice. I don't want to put on more, what with all the pudding you give me.

—Look at you, skinny as a hound's tooth. A brisk wind and you wouldn't have to pay for a holiday, you could set off from the top of Trellick Towers, be there by breakfast.

—You're so wrong.

—Got nothing to worry about, love, she said, and then I spooned tart into my mouth and forgot anyone else was there. I fell back against the sofa, closed my eyes.

—What do you think?

—It's gorgeous, Ida. Truthfully, you've excelled.

—Amazing, Wills said, mouth full, and he meant it.

—So, what do you do with yourself, Wills? Ida asked.

He stared, chewing, until we were shifting in our seats. He swallowed.

—Wills is looking for work, I said. I'm going to help him find a job while he stays here.

—What kind of work?

—Uh . . . IT? he said. I wanna get into studio engineering, but I don't know how. Yet.

—Oh.

Ida wanted to say more, forced her mouth closed. She didn't listen to music.

We talked amongst ourselves for the rest of the evening, Wills watching TV, chipping in with a half-smile, or an occasional mumbled agreement. I kept my eyes on my neighbor, though she seemed to ignore him after her tentative inquiries, and we mostly talked about Graham and her three granddaughters, how happy she was that they were coming. Wills ate the majority of the Bakewell tart, going back to the kitchen whenever his current slice was finished. I thought Ida might have something to say while he was gone, but she would fall silent and we would sit that way, the comforting babble of TV filling the gap, and something felt right about those moments, I could think to myself, *My son's in the kitchen cutting a slice of Bakewell tart*, and it felt right, despite the niggling wrong of the day. I think I needed that: to forget my doubts and relax. It had been a long time since I could, and the calm lasted even through the shouts outside, yet I was soon brought back to reality and I sighed.

—Bloody kids, Ida said. She poured another glass of sherry. To think I was similar.

—We all were, I said.

—Not you, love, she laughed. Not you.

—I had my moments. Nothing like them, or you, but I had them.

—To moments, Ida said, raising her glass.

—You're a one, I told her, lifting mine. You really are.

When the night thickened and Ida was leaving, we stood by the open door. I touched her hand.

—Thanks. I appreciate you coming over, you know that.

—Now let's not get all misty.

—And I know you made that monkey story up. But thanks anyway.

—You're clever, she said, grasping my hand. Just don't be too clever for your own good.

—I'm sure you'll tell me if I am.

Ida winked, squeezed my fingers. Then she was off down the landing. I waited until she went inside her flat, shut the door.

❦

Screams first. A familiar rustle like whispering schoolchildren, a crackle on the edge of my hearing. Harsh breath, right beside me. Then something penetrated oily gloom, tiny sparks of firefly lights, and I could see, I was running, dream sister beside me, hair flat against her temples as though glued to both sides, skin glistening from sweat and the glow of lights, which were everywhere.

"Come nuh," she said, throat dry, and I was entranced by the sound of the words until she tugged my wrist hard enough to feel pain burst in my shoulder. I wanted to snatch my hand away, did that, and then the screams became louder and something registered, and before I could come to terms with what I was hearing my dream sister was gone, swallowed by bushes that chanted a surreptitious chorus in harmony with the voice of the wind. I followed, darting into foliage, ignoring sharp needles of leaves on my arms and legs, ignoring the heat and screams and the rush of air and noise, just running, chasing without seeing, leaping and ducking, head low, forehead pointed in the direction of her noisy progress.

It went on that way, the screaming from behind us, the crackle and pops, the sounds of our breathing, the crash of breaking leaves, the thump of my heart and the desperate thought that if I lost my dream sister I would lose myself, when I stumbled into a clearing. No, not even stumbled; I actually fell, scraping my knees on soft earth, rum dark, bald of grass. I saw the rear of my dream sister's knees, a curved indent lit by moonlight, saw her torn skirt and blouse, black streaks of grime on her clothes, before I realized she was looking up, head tilted as though drinking from an oversized jug. I tracked her sight, on hands and knees, wondering what she was looking at.

It was the cane.

They were huge, more like bamboo than sugarcane, as round as a tall man's thigh, chattering as they clashed in the wind. The chatter rose louder, died. My dream sister spun, faced me, eyes like inverted night sky, moon white on the outside, pitch black in the center.

"Dem comin," she whispered. I wanted to tell her not to talk that way, Mama wouldn't allow it, and then I heard them. And I turned.

The night sky behind us was ablaze. Orange light, thick smoke, the crackling louder now, more like a roar, and the heat wasn't just the normal heat of night, it was a fire, it was howling, and it came from our house. I couldn't see over the bushes and trees, but instinct told me: it was our house. The house was on fire because Papa had done something to McIntyre.

I recalled screaming, the voice. My mother's. I pictured things being done, too raw for a child's knowledge, but I wasn't a child, was I? I was seeing through a child's eyes but my mind still belonged to me, didn't it? It felt that way as I heard her shriek inside my head, saw her surrounded by men holding gas lamps and torches and dogs, watching one of their number sit between her legs, rip off clothes, fight her beating hands, laugh, display rotten teeth. And the dogs barked and pulled at leashes, growled, and strained their noses at the dark grass, the bush, in the direction of us.

Echoing barks rolled across the night sky. She was right, they had caught our scent and they were coming.

"You hear dem?" she said, poised on toes, eyes darting. I nodded. "Den leh we go . . ."

Pushing aside the giant cane was like pushing through the legs of adults; the stalks were reluctant, resistant, holding ground. It was harder work than the bush, and it seemed as though the fire was coming closer, as it grew hotter by the second, and the barking got louder, from every angle, and my dream sister seemed disoriented as she hesitated, and I knew we couldn't go on for much longer. Sometimes I would look up and the highest knots of cane were somehow familiar, they seemed to have thin, pinched faces, like the whittled grimace of weathered African masks, and when I noticed that I felt like they had seen me too, were trying to tell me something. I stepped closer and it was then I heard it, a soft language, low and deep, and I saw bitter smiles above. I elbowed past my dream sister when the feeling came, I laughed and took her hand, and then I was tugging her through the chatter of wood as she flailed and tried to keep up. I ran, head tilted upward, looking into the faces of the cane, not at the ground, not behind me where I could hear the dogs more clearly, but at dark seed eyes and pursed lips, which leaned toward me as I moved, told me which way to turn in deep, melodious

African voices, which led me further into the field, parted to allow me access, chattered in approval when I passed.

My dream sister faltered. She looked at the cane, mouth open. She snatched her hand away. She looked at me and shook her head. I wanted to call out, but the dogs came. Huge, powerful beasts, sand-colored fur, scarred backs, foaming with sweat, teeth reflecting moonlight. They leaped on her and she screamed, went down. I ran.

I could hear the dogs tear at her, rip meat from bone, and her screams, which turned my sweat cold, caused steam to pour from my body. My dream sister had bought me time. The cane parted before I even got to them, closed behind me, and it was easy to see where to go, it was just a case of following an open path into blackness. I ran into something solid, with give, bounced forward and back. Struggled. I was stuck, seemingly by my body. Arms, legs, torso, I couldn't move. Only my head had escaped; I could turn right, left, up. If I were to look down I would be stuck that way, attached by the forehead to whatever had caught me. I strained my chin upward, my head back, to see.

The web was made of a gossamer-like material but thicker, more transparent, large glass noodles. Milk white, it hung between two stalks of cane, the biggest yet, solitary sentries as thick as branchless oaks. It stretched across the path in the center of a crossroads. The earth beneath me was iron red. Coming from the right or left, I might have bumped into cane, but from the direction I'd been running there was no way around, no way to see it was there.

I had seen the structure before. Not in the park, or a

fairy tale, but inside the head of a human being. It was the *arachnoid mater*, the spider mother, that transparent guardian of the brain.

I struggled harder as I heard the barking resume. The web was sticky, almost painful, and it felt as though I would risk tearing my skin to break free. I looked at the path, the crossroads, to see if anything else could help, and noticed the other thing, a dance of reflected fire and moonlight further along the path, two equal rows of light, like this:

:::

The lights rose and fell in slow rhythm. There was no sound apart from the constant voice of the fire, the sharp bark of dogs. Fear seeped into me. For there to be a web, something had spun it. For the web to be that huge, something huge created it. I started to gasp, wondered if the cane had misled me. When I looked at the sentinels, their knotted faces were impassive, staring straight ahead like any soldier would. I thought I saw vague movement, a twitch in the brow, a hardening of features, but it was difficult to tell.

The barks were louder, almost upon me. I struggled as much as I dared without hurting myself. Concluded I might have to if I was to escape. The lights began to grow obvious, not exactly bigger, but clearer. The beast came into view.

Matted, sticky fur, a smell of wet clothes. A rumble of breathing that made me tremble. Long black fur at the maw, overhanging fangs like shortened cane stalks. The creature ambled from the protection of the shadows into the light of the natural clearing formed by the crossroads. I screamed as her eyes turned toward me, and the barking grew louder, and the spider got as close as the sentinel to my right, within reaching distance, and the smell was overpowering, nauseating. I retched as she leaned back on four legs. I closed my eyes, tried not to think about the pain. There was a rush of something next to me and I jumped, shuddered a cry, heard the bark of the dog become a whine, a howl, and my back was struck by hot liquid and soon the dogs were quiet, all of them, and there was nothing but wind and fire, even the insects of night fell into silence.

The snuffle of the beast, crunch of bones, earth scraping against flesh. I assumed the bodies were being dragged. I was shivering, cold even though the heat was unbearable. The spider returned, body radiating warmth I could feel, and I tensed, but it moved away before I even trembled. She walked, spinnerets dangling like teats, back into the overhanging shadow of the cane. She stopped. Turned until all eight eyes faced me. I hung in her web, arms and legs outstretched, static as a portrait, and she stayed in place, not moving, not eating, breathing soft and shallow, watching me.

❦

I was woken by something, some noise. Lay under warm sheets trying to shake away the dream. It took awhile. The ferocity, the residue of fear, my own morbid imagination. I practiced inhaling deep, holding it in. When I was breathing slower I got up, went into the living room. Wills had his toes pushed under the sofa and was doing rapid sit-ups in boxer shorts and a vest. His skinny body was lined with muscles. The television was tuned to a radio station pumping house music. I rubbed my eyes.

—Good morning.

—Mornin, he said, still crunching. All right?

—Yes, thanks. You sleep okay on that sofa?

—Fine, thanks.

—I'm thinking of clearing the spare room. You can have some privacy.

—Yeah? He puffed. Cool. Made bacon. In the oven.

—That's kind of you.

I went into the kitchen. It was a mess. There was a pot of beans on the stove, a used frying pan in the sink, and the cutting board had half a loaf of bread protruding from the wrapper, surrounded by a debris of crumbs. I stared. The phone rang. I went back into the living room to get it. He was still crunching. He must have done at least twenty since I'd left, and he showed no signs of stopping.

—Hello?

—Beverley.

Damn. Last thing I needed. I took the cordless into the bedroom.

—Morning, Jackie.

—Good morning. How's everything?

—All right. You?

—We're fine, thanks. I was just calling to ask if you've seen that boy and what the situation is. I was talking with Frank and we think it's quite dangerous for you to be alone if some unstable child is following you, so we were thinking—

—He came back, Jackie. I let him in. He's here right now. He's staying.

She couldn't quite take that in. It temporarily robbed her of speech.

—Beverley, I'm not sure that's the best course—

—He's my *son*, Jackie. Or at least he might be. There is such a thing as benefit of the doubt.

—And your evidence is?

I bit my lip, fumed.

—We're coming. We'll be there in a few hours.

—Jackie, there's no—

—If you're right, he's our nephew. We're coming, okay?

—Okay.

—See you soon.

She hung up. I swore at the duvet. Wills was standing in my doorway, vest soaked, towel wrapped around his neck like a serpent.

—Hey.

—Hey, I said, getting up.

—Who's that?

—You're aunt and uncle, I told him. They're coming over.

I wanted to leave, but he was blocking the way. His eyes seemed flat, reptilian. I hadn't noticed before. He was holding the towel at both ends and his biceps were larger than I'd thought. Strangely enough, he reminded me of Patrick. Similar build, same complexion, darker than mine, same way of standing. That should have reassured me.

—You all right?

—Not really. Jackie can be a royal pain. We've never got on, but it's worse these days. Thank God you don't have siblings, I said, and heard myself. His arms dropped by his sides. His posture deflated. Sorry.

—No worries, he said to the floor. So, would you like to eat?

—Yes. I was going to talk about that. You see—

The buzzer sounded, loud, a rasping hum.

—What?

—I'd better get that.

I slid past him to the intercom. I was trying to dismiss the look I'd seen, the expression I was used to. The club had trained me. I didn't want to admit what I saw written on his face. He followed me into the living room.

—What, you don't want breakfast?

—It's not that, it's just . . . Hold on a second. I picked up the handset. Hello, who is it?

—Miss, it's Sam. Are you busy?

—Oh. How are you?

—I'm all right, miss. I come wiv Hayley and Chris, is that cool?

—Sure. No problem. I'll let you in.

I took the phone from my ear, pressed the entry button. I could hear the door clang open and received another quick flash of my previous dream, Papa at work at the anvil, pounding red metal. I leaned against the wall.

—Beverley? You don't want breakfast then?

I came back to the room, the boy.

—It's not that. It's just, you left quite a mess, and I know you mean well, but I hate an untidy kitchen and—

—It's okay . . . Vicks used to say the same ting. I'll clean it.

Something lay beneath his words, some hardness. I

watched the contraction and release of his muscles as he stalked into the kitchen. I didn't want to follow but I couldn't help myself, my feet took me to the threshold of that tiny space he dominated by size alone. Dishes and pots came together and I winced.

—You don't have to do it now.

—You got people comin, innit, he said, without looking back. I'll make tea.

—Thank you, I replied. The letter box barked. I'll just go answer the door.

My kids were on the landing, three serious faces. They walked into the living room and waited. That threw me. They had been to my flat before, many times. I operated an open-door policy for my kids and their friends. Sometimes there was homework done on my living room floor, a documentary or feature. I even tried to make them watch foreign films, though they hated subtitles. Occasionally one was kicked out of their home and my sofa bed became theirs until they found a hostel, or made up with the parents, or moved in with their partner. That's when I realized that none of the three had seen the sofa extended into a bed. They were looking at rumpled sheets, at Wills's tote bag, listening to the shrill sounds of kitchen utensils.

—Sorry, didn't know you had someone over, Sam said, shifting from sneaker to sneaker.

—Yes, we're just getting up. How are you guys?

Nods and mutters, hands in pockets.

—Just thought we'd pass, see how you are, miss, Hayley said. You said you was under the weather.

—Gotta look after you, miss . . . Chris grinned.

—Thanks for the thought, but I'm fine, really. Actually, I have people coming, and I was going to get ready to go out too, but you're welcome to stay until then. Oh!

I brightened, remembering.

—Whassat, miss?

Sam avoiding my eye, making me nervous.

—I've been thinking of clearing out my spare room, moving some boxes and bringing the laptop and printer in here, if that's at all possible. I was going to get Wills, my lodger, to do it, but I'm sure he'd love a hand.

—Your lodger, miss? Hayley said.

—It's a recent thing, quite sudden. Could you help?

—Yeah, course, Sam broke in when the others didn't say anything. They were looking around the flat, at Wills's clothes, the tote, the bedsheets. I had the strangest feeling, overriding what they were actually doing, and I began to think their actions reminded me of Vicky. There was very little surprise. I sat on the arm of the sofa and pulled my dressing gown closed over my T-shirt.

—That's good. It'd be an enormous help. It shouldn't take long.

Wills came in. My kids grew rigid. He moved slower, gave me the tea.

—Thanks. Wills, this is Sam, Hayley, and Chris, some of my after-school kids. Guys, this is Wills.

Their faces, animated. Sam's closed like a fist. Chris sizing Wills up. Hayley doing the same, a tiny smile. Wills, blank as ever, putting down the towel, reaching for his T-shirt.

—Hi, said Hayley. Sam glared.

—What's good? Wills said, snaking into his clothes.

—You don't have to get dressed for us—

—Yes, fam, Sam said, offering his palm, cutting Hayley off. Chris did the same. Wills slapped both, looked at me.

—Kitchen's done, he said. I heard you talk about the spare room.

—Yes. If you can make space, it's yours.

—No problem.

—We'll give you a hand, Sam intoned, gruff, already moving.

The others walked behind him. I went too, carrying my tea, peeking over broad shoulders. There wasn't much in the room: a desk, a single bed, piled boxes of summer clothing and shoes, empties that once contained the TV and my laptop, duvet covers, a few books and knickknacks never used. They were staring, probably wishing they hadn't said yes. Sam was leading and that was strange.

—If you could leave the desk and bring those boxes into the living room, that'd be great, I told them. That should clear enough space, Wills, don't you think?

—Yeah, sure.

—I'll make lemonade. Ida brought a Bakewell tart last night.

Low mumbles of appreciation. I frowned, left the room.

It didn't take long to squeeze the juice and come back with a jug filled with ice and cloudy lemonade, a cluster of glasses. The spare room was almost bare, my living room filled with boxes. The kids seemed to work well together. Chris was most verbose, attempting to make conversation with Wills, something that proved quite a challenge. Hayley acted shy; she blushed whenever Wills came close and that bothered Sam, it was easy to tell. His lip was pushed out, teeth set. I wondered what the story was, whether they were actually seeing each other. Wills lifted and carried as though he was alone, mannequin blank, ignoring Hayley, responding to Chris with respect and very few words. He readily stepped aside when he crossed paths with Sam, even though he towered over him. Everyone could feel the atmosphere. Sitting in the living room drinking lemonade, perched in whatever space we could find. Chris gave me a measured look, lifted his eyebrows toward Sam and shook his head without the others noticing.

—So where shall we put the boxes then? Hayley asked.

—In the bedroom. Anywhere, really, I can sort them out later. I should probably give most of it away. I haven't looked at the stuff in years.

—We could do that, Chris offered.

—That would be nice. I'll let you know when I've gone through them.

—Good lemonade, Wills said, out of the blue. The others frowned.

—Not too sweet, not too tangy, Chris agreed, lifting his glass and inspecting the contents. Sam laughed. What's up wid you?

—Nuttin, man, Sam said. Shall we get movin?

—All right, Major Tom, Hayley said, and this time it was Wills who laughed. For some reason that unsettled everyone; maybe it was the sound, loud and high, more like a giggle. Sam was sneering.

—Anyway, come we go, he said, rougher than I was used to. Man's got tings to do.

They carried the boxes into my bedroom and

dumped them by the door. By then I just wanted them to leave before my sister came; that would be too much by anyone's reckoning. Wills said he was going to tidy the spare room, move his bag from the living room, get himself ready to go out. My kids, driven by Sam's eagerness to depart, made their way outside. I asked whether they had completed the homework for class and about their families, normal conversation. When Hayley and Chris went onto the landing, Sam stopped, pushed the door closed. They didn't come back, but I could hear their voices. A setup.

—Everything all right?

—Yeah, miss. Just wanted to make sure *you* were, y'get me?

—What do you mean?

—Wiv this yout. Everyting cool?

—Yes, of course. Why wouldn't it be?

—I dunno.

Hands in pockets, back against the wall. It was dark in my small corridor, difficult to see.

—Sam. Come on. What are you trying to say?

—You shouldn't let strange youts in yuh gates, miss. You don't know him.

I sighed, mouth closed.

—I know what you're saying. And I know you mean well. But this is my business, Sam. Not yours, or Chris and Hayley's, or Ida's.

I was only testing my theory, but he still flinched.

—Miss, man . . .

—Seriously. Don't let her get you with gossip. She's my best friend and she means well too, but you can't trust everything she says.

—Well, you can't trust him either. Man's dodgy, I don't need Ida to see, he whispered, expression severe. You can't.

—All right, Sam, I said, and opened the door. Hayley and Chris were as close as they could get without touching wood. I gestured toward the landing. See you at the club.

Sam bowed his head, walked. I stepped outside and there she was, pretending to sweep her already clean doorstep.

—Morning, Ida.

—Mornin, love! Everything okay?

—Lovely, thanks! I turned to my kids. Thanks for coming over and helping with the room. See you soon.

—Bye, miss!

They walked, heads low, crowding each other, Ida trying not to watch until they hit the stairs, and then trying not to watch me, just continuing to sweep. I smiled at nothing. Hummed Harriott. Looked over the landing wall to see them and caught my sister parking, saw the kids march past her and away, saw her get out and look around the cul-de-sac, shake her head, say something to Frank that made him nod and also look left to right. I backed away, steel-eyed. The sweeping had stopped.

—Your sister, innit?

—Yes. That's Jackie.

—Been awhile.

—I'd better let her in, I said, and went inside. They took a long time getting to the intercom. I paced, four repetitive steps, trying to piece my story together, told myself it wasn't a story—it was *truth*. I had nothing to hide, nothing to fear, even though I heard a distant thud in my ears. The buzzer went.

—Hi, Jackie. Front door's open.

I sat on the folded sofa. I was angry, trying not to be. Then I remembered the boy. Wills. Or Malakay. My son.

The room had been emptied of anything relating to him. I got up and went into the spare room. He wasn't there, but the tote was. I found him in the kitchen, by the fridge, reading a Post-it note.

—That's funny, he said.

—What's that?

—*Happiness often sneaks in from a door you left open . . .* John Barrymore. He lifted the paper with a finger. I like that.

—Notes to self, I said. Past me to future me. I write them, try to forget them, and when I need them most, they find me.

—They're all over the place.

—Yes.

—I like that. You think.

—I try. It helps.

Light slanted through the kitchen window and onto his face, and I saw what Hayley had, that he was handsome, and I was proud, even though the notion was silly. I had no reason, just simple hope.

—I'm gonna get washed, go see Vicky.

—Okay. Jackie and Frank are here. You can meet them when you come out, but no pressure. Honestly.

—Cool.

—Take your time, I said, and went to greet them. They were stepping into the flat slowly. They didn't notice me. I cleared my throat.

—Aha, Frank said. The woman herself!

I feigned a smile, crossed the room.

—Frank. Too, too long.

—Isn't it? He sang in that high voice of his, a heavy hand on my shoulder.

—Hello, Beverley.

—Hi, Jackie.

We kissed, almost-touches on both cheeks, regarded each other. Frank was smiling like a lunatic. I've always thought them a strange combination: my sister tall, buxom in her advancing age, if that's not unfair, thin dreadlocks pulled back to reveal a coastal hairline, pale, creamy skin; Frank short and broad everywhere, body, hands, head, completely bald, thick glasses, always dressed the same, knitted sweaters and shirts, corduroys. They were lecturers at the same university, where Frank taught math, Jackie art history. When they'd first met my sister had been thrilled to date a man who didn't have FM on his car radio, just like her.

—How are you both?

—Oh, fine, fine . . .

—Do make yourself at home.

They followed. I could almost feel them wince, their bodies closed and huddled, cramped by lack of space.

—You've done the place up.

—Awhile ago, yes. Would you like a drink?

—No thanks. We're not stopping.

—Oh.

Frank pointed at the ceiling. I thought something was there until I realized he was asking a question.

—Do you have rose hip?

Jackie gave him a look.

—I said we weren't stopping.

—Well, if the man wants rose hip, I said. The smile dropped from my face when she fixed me with thin eyes. I picked it up, turned to Frank. I do, I said. Let me put the kettle on.

A brief walk to the kitchen, a flick of the switch and count to ten before I went back, straightened my dressing gown.

—Still fixing the flat up?

—Rearranging. Making space, I said.

—Is he here?

Frank trying not to look.

—In the bathroom. Taking a shower.

—And you? Jackie said.

—I don't think my hygiene is your concern.

—Now ladies, Frank said, sitting forward. Let's not regress. We're here because there's a chance, however slight, that something wonderful has happened. God knows there's been enough hurt.

—Quite right, Jackie said.

—And before we begin, I'd just like to say how pleased I am that you called us. I've been telling your sister for years it's time to mend our bridges, and I think this is a marvelous opportunity to reconnect, discuss our differences, patch up whatever grievances we've had.

—I don't have any grievances.

He coughed, glanced at Jackie.

—Come now. That can't be true.

—It is. I'm fine with the fact that you'd rather avoid dealing with me and get on with your own lives. I'm fine that you left me to stew for all those years, that you think everything I've done since is a complete waste of time. I've accepted that, a lot of other things too. If that's the way it is, it is. I'm not upset, which is why I called in the first place. Whatever happened, you have a right to know.

—Well, if that's how you feel, I can't correct you, but I do sense a great deal of unexplored animosity.

I stood up.

—Rose hip, you said? Frank opened his mouth, didn't speak. I'll get it.

While I made tea, I heard the bathroom door open and close, footsteps into the spare room. I carried the hot mug back on a saucer. They were whispering, heads low.

—There you go, I said. Sugar's right here.

—Thank you so much. Now Beverley, none of us want to get off on the wrong foot—

—It's fine, Frank. You're right. We do have a lot of ground to cover. I was just hoping we could do all that another day, especially since we're pressed for time.

—We've been talking about that. I think we can make an exception.

Jackie moved her head up and down. It seemed to have tripled in weight if her actions were to be believed. I was mesmerized, almost too much to speak. I wanted to watch her head bob like a toy dog in a rear window.

—Well, I appreciate that.

—It's no trouble. You two are all you have left, you know, that's got to mean something. Your parents would be proud.

Nails dug into the soft flesh of my palm; my slippers were bunched at the toes. I released, made myself relax. Jackie's head was tilted in a listening pose. Her eyes glistened.

—I've had a chance to think, and I've concluded that we've done Mum and Dad a major disservice. I promised I'd take care of you. I know I haven't done my best, and you resent me—

—We don't have to do this, I told her again. Not today.

—I'm trying to say I don't blame you.

I wanted to ask, *For what, misplacing my son?* Didn't.

—And I don't blame you either. But I hardly think we need to discuss that now. I'm more concerned with my son. And it's unfair for us to—

—You should hear what she has to say, Frank broke in. It's very important for you both to air things out. Think of this as a preface.

He sat back, pleased.

—I understand, but another time maybe? That's what I was thinking. Malakay's going out soon, and if you stayed maybe we could—

—Frank has a class. And I have grading to do. My point is, we want to be here for you, Beverley, we don't want you to look outside the family for help. Of course, that might be good for you once in a while, but for the most part your support should come from us.

—Exactly, Frank said. He beamed.

—I'm not sure what you mean.

—Let me explain, Jackie said, leaning forward, hands placed sideways as if holding an unseen box, and then her eyes slid over my shoulder. Wills was there, behind me. I got up.

—Hey, come on in, sit down.

—You sure? I don't wanna disturb you lot . . .

—It's okay. You can sit by me.

I could feel his crackle of nerves as he brushed past to sit with his knees together beside me. He wouldn't meet anyone's eye. And I tried not to see him as they did: high-top sneakers complete with protruding tongue, formerly white soles dark with grime. Drooping jeans, thick cuffs, garish T-shirt proclaiming the designer's name in huge letters, oversized jacket, yellow of all colors—why yellow? The matching baseball hat perched on top of wild, unruly hair. And it was nothing out of the ordinary, abnormal, or abrasive, they must have seen a hundred kids dressed that way on the journey to my flat, but I could sense them recoil without even looking, I could hear the horror in their silence, and it was all I could do not to throw my arms around him and bury him in flesh, shield him so he wouldn't have to see the thoughts projected from their eyes, that confusion, supposition, the abhorrence and critical sense of knowing that my kids spoke of sometimes, but I had never seen. It was alive and dancing in their faces like an imp, undeniable. I felt empty space, and I had to fight every nerve in my body, force them not to send a lightning-quick message to my brain, cause it to reply by saying, *Make space, move away, create distance*.

Their backs were straight, hands clasped, closer to each other. I didn't want to see. Icy dismay flooded the heat which preceded it. A flush, Sue would have said.

—Everybody, this is Wills, I smiled, and they jerked at the sound of my voice. Wills, this is Jackie and Frank.

—Hello, Wills, Jackie said, evenly.

—Hello, said Frank.

—Hey.

—How are you doing today?

Jackie's voice higher than normal, slow. My eyes closed.

—Fine, thanks.

—This must be very strange for you, Frank told him. Wills didn't answer. Beverley tells us you've been waiting to speak with her for quite awhile.

—Why is that? Jackie said, and she hesitated, took a quick breath. What I mean is, what brought you to the conclusion that you should be here?

—That's an odd question, I said. One we all know the answer to.

—Yes, said Frank, and I was grateful because his tone was softer than before. But I think we'd like to know why Wills thinks he's here. The evidence, if he wouldn't mind.

Halting pigeon song, somewhere on the landing. Everyone listened, aware of the quiet.

—Documents, Wills said.

—I beg your pardon?

Jackie's eyebrows rose.

—Documents, innit? I got documents to prove.

—Prove what?

Frank on the edge of the sofa. Jackie's head bowed, eyes lifted.

—I was snatched. When I was a baby, he took me.

—Who, Wills?

—Hey, hey, take it easy, I said.

—We have to ask.

From Jackie, stiff hand raised in my direction, severe again.

—Yes, but it's not an interrogation.

—It's all right. Wills looked away. He had a load of stuff. Newspapers, baby clothes. Pictures of my mum.

I clutched at my palms. Outside a car horn beeped, a man's voice said, *Fuck off*, drawing out each word. Jackie twitched.

—You mean Beverley?

—Yeah.

—Any birth certificates, hospital name tags?

—Why would he have those?

—Beverley. Frank's mouth twitched, a disappointed twist. You don't have to be like that. You're not helping.

—Well, neither are you. Last I heard, you're not a qualified detective.

—And what is the position of the police here? Jackie asked the room. I cursed. She noticed. You haven't told them?

—We need to figure things out.

—You haven't told them.

—I don't think it's a good idea, Wills said, and I almost kicked him.

—Oh, you don't? Jackie looked at him. They had similarly shaped eyes, as far as I could tell; thin, oval. Tell us why you don't think it's a good idea.

His head fell.

—This is useless, I said.

—Beverley, wait. You called us and we came—

—Not for this. Not this.

—I'm rather confused, Frank said. I could see he wasn't the only one. Wills had raised his head, and was trying to place the accent with the man, failing. You say a man kidnapped you and kept you all this time, along with newspaper clippings about the abduction?

—Yeah.

Sneering, snatching looks, baseball cap hiding face.

—And he just kept them lying around for you to find?

—Don't be stupid.

Indrawn breath. Wide eyes.

—Pardon me?

—Don't be stupid, innit? They were locked away in a big trunk. In his room. He said weird stuff and I got suspicious, he'd always been funny about the trunk, kept it locked. I bust it open and found stuff.

—You broke in?

—Yeah, I broke in, he said, glaring at Frank.

—Can you describe this man? Jackie said, and all of a sudden I'd had enough.

—Look, this isn't what I had in mind. I think you'd better come back another day.

—Beverley, Frank said, showing me palms.

—Shut up. This has nothing to do with you, I'm talking to Jackie. You're not achieving anything. I think you should leave.

I got to my feet. So did Jackie, and eventually Frank too. Wills ignored them, the peak of his cap pointed at their feet.

—I'm wondering what you intend with all this, Jackie said. You're clearly not rational. None of this makes the remotest sense.

—You must call the police. Frank's voice was keening, high. It's the only way. I've a good mind to do it for you.

—Do, and I'll never speak to you again. Either of you.

—We might be willing to take that risk, Jackie said.

At that point I ceased caring, stepped toward them.

—Out. Right now.

—Thanks for the tea, Frank said, and then they were shuffling toward the door, me close behind.

—We're coming back, Jackie warned, before I slammed the door.

I went back into the living room.

—That wasn't about you.

The peak raised. His eyes were red, but he wasn't crying. Fingers writhed in his lap.

—I better go.

—It wasn't, honestly.

—Vicky won't wait if I'm not there a certain time. I would have gone all the way fuh nuttin. She's probably gone.

—How are you getting there?

—Walking.

—No you're not.

I went into the bedroom, rooted in my purse. All I had was a twenty, so I gave it to him. He looked at the note as though it was stuck to his fingers.

—I can't.

—Yes you can. Get an Oyster at least, buy yourself fish and chips.

A tear trickled down his cheek.

—I'm really sorry.

—It's okay. I'll see you later.

—You take care, I whispered.

Wills left. The door closed with a soft click.

❧

Reality is pain. What determines real in the outside world is defined by electrical impulses that make contact with our nerves, and in turn our brains. What determines pain in our bodies is defined by electrical impulses that make contact with our nerves, and in turn our brains. How we perceive the world, both inner and outer, is grossly affected by how we are hardwired as human beings. We experience the world this way because we are built to. Reality is pain.

❧

I had my appointment with Sue, so I got washed and ready and made my way. She answered the door in a sober manner, saying little. In the office that wasn't really one, she sat and listened. I wasn't sure what to tell her, and if it hadn't been for the confidentiality agreement I wouldn't have said a word.

—That's it? she said when I'd been quiet for some time.

—That's quite a lot, I replied, and she nodded. She thought for a while, knee bouncing. She was dressed attractively: black boots, cream tights, and a plaid skirt that fit her slim figure well.

—I don't have to say I think you've made a big mistake.

—Cute way to remind me.

—I'm serious. No jokes. You don't know this boy.

—So everyone keeps saying.

—Okay. You're fully aware. So can I be frank?

—Yes. Please.

—Let's just say he is your son.

—Okay.

—For twenty years he's been brought up in someone else's care. That person, or people—forgive me, but I'm being frank here—quite probably abused him.

—Yes.

—Which probably contributed to him being expelled from not just one school, but many.

—Yes.

—After which he was placed in a pupil referral unit where it's very likely he was either subjected to, or carried out, further abuse.

—We don't know that, but yes, for the purposes of your theory, let's assume you're correct.

—Then he was ejected into the world, where he ends up in a supervised youth hostel and later finds evidence that suggests he was abducted as a child, and the people he believed to be his abusive parents are in fact liars, and his real parents are out there somewhere, with no knowledge of who he is and what's become of him. A fair assessment?

—Very.

—So, bearing all this in mind, wouldn't you think that this boy—this vulnerable, fragile boy—is more than likely pretty disturbed?

—That would be true, yes.

—And the fact that a boy with possible mental health issues is staying in your home doesn't bother you in the slightest?

—Of course. But I'm his mother. I've abandoned him before.

—You didn't abandon him, Beverley.

—You know what I mean.

Sue was thinking, watching, tapping her foot harder.

—If he isn't your son, the same rules apply, you know.

I tried to stay upright, couldn't, and slumped.

—Yes, I said, quieter.

—Who knows what he could do. What he's done over the years. What's in his files, whether he may already have been diagnosed.

I squirmed. I was the soft creature without a shell, exposed.

—And if he was some boarding-school graduate?

—The same rules would apply.

I clutched the armrests, breathing hard.

—Beverley. This isn't good. For you.

I saw her check my nails. They were rough, long. I hadn't noticed.

—What are you saying?

—That you're going through what anyone would. That you need to slow down. Think. Don't take yourself backward. You have a choice. You can deal with this; you just need to give yourself a chance.

The gloss of her boots, crossed legs, foot bouncing. Very slow, up and down. I counted time, took a deep breath.

—I can do this. I can. There's just so much doubt.

—There is. That's also normal.

—I want to run.

—Oh, you can't do that. I'm afraid you're going to have to see this through. Have you spoken to Seth?

I shook my head. I didn't want her to see what I couldn't explain.

—You must. He cares about you. He'll help.

—All right.

—And if you'd like me to see you both, you and Wills, that won't be a problem.

—Really? I said.

◈

Time is running and running and passing.

◈

Bright midday sun, unbroken blue. A cold breeze that swept through the body, causing us to sway as much with the gentle force of nature as to keep warm. Hands in pockets, scarves and gloves. Feathered hats, dark suits. And the singing. Oh God, the singing. Voices as much a part of me as my breath, or my lungs, voices that recalled black velvet on walls, the imprint of fluorescent parishes, islands. Tiny Venetian glasses embossed with gold, matching plates, the low creak of plastic on cream sofas. Gone now, forever gone, but the voices are with us, they remain, rising and falling like bitter wind, shaping who we were, who we are. *Rock of Ages. Abide with Me. Onward Christian Soldiers.* The young holding hymn books and pamphlets, elders reciting from memory, the sweet sound of joined voices, women overpowering men, leading the way with strident tones, nasal and high, men weaving baritones beneath, a tapestry of sound, beautiful harmony that resonated, shook me, made me smile even as tears fell, even as I raised my face to the light, even as the abrupt sound of the spade ripped into earth, ripped into me, and I fell against Ida, and she held me, and cradled me, and though I buried my head in her thick fur coat it was all I could do not to feel joy, because it was beautiful and ours.

The sharp call of the spade joined by others. I forced my head to rise. The women continued to sing while the men worked with the compact, sinewy sextons, digging and lifting, lifting and throwing. Frank was there, mud on shoes, jacketless, shirt rolled to elbows. Patrick too, tears falling as he pushed, placed a foot on heaped mud, pulled. Jackie stood to one side, Frank's jacket hung on one arm, staring at the grave. I wandered over, mouth moving, grabbed a pile of mud, and hefted. Threw. Jackie came to my side. She grabbed a pile, threw. We wailed, held each other. It felt good.

I let Jackie go. Walked to a sexton, gestured for his spade. He seemed dumbfounded but handed it to me without argument, and I pushed into the earth, relished the shudder of connection, the tingle in my arms. Lifted. Everyone was looking. There was another crunch of a spade close beside me, and when I turned it was Jackie, wearing a grim, down-turned smile. We dug and threw, threw and dug. More spades, the sextons outgunning us with a pace that was difficult to believe let alone match, yet they eyed us without a smile and nodded, eyes blue as sky, sweat dripping onto earth, and we kept going until we were sweating with them. And the singing went on. High notes and low, loud and soft, patient and everlasting as the ocean, the singing went on and we buried my father.

Even when the reverend said his final words, Father still managed to surprise us. There we were, in the center of the looming Victorian cemetery, in mourning by the plot occupied by his father before him, and his mother, and mine, far from any walls or houses, when a rich smell of curry goat began to rise, and the mourners began to look at one another, half-smiling, confused. Everyone knew it was his favorite dish. Even the reverend, who didn't, was frowning and looking over his shoulder, Bible in hand, eulogy forgotten as the smell grew stronger. Jackie laughed, cried. Frank shook his head, looked upward, and Patrick's eyes met mine with the tiniest hint of a smile, new wife a smudge of out-of-focus beauty, and a shiver went through me, not of fear or cold, but because it would happen.

The community hall, eating before trestle tables. When the time for speeches came, the photographer asked to speak.

"And we all smelled the curry *rise* over the congregation, so you know he reached the better place, ah!" he said, dark face and white teeth, still chewing.

He received the longest applause. Frank got up to support Jackie, who had taken the microphone and was beginning to stand. I slipped into the corridor, upstairs to the room with all the coats. Fumbled for my pack of Embassy, opened a window. A temporary habit, only a few years, and I always knew I'd give up.

The door swung toward me. I jumped.

"Hello there."

He'd caught me sitting on a spare table, half-turned, blowing smoke from the window. I stubbed the cigarette against brick, let it fall. It's a wonder I didn't burn the place down.

"Patrick."

"You don't have to stop. Jackie told me you smoke."

"It's only a puff."

Patrick came nearer. It was written all over his face,

mine too I have to admit. Had been at the graveside; what would Father have said?

"Where's Rachelle?"

"In the car. She knows I have to say my goodbyes."

"When are you leaving?"

"Tomorrow night," he said, looking at muddy shoes. "Eight."

He kneeled in front of me. There was more gray, less hair. I reached for him, stroked his head.

"Be quick."

"No," he said, and took off my shoes. "I won't. They can wait."

"Rachelle?"

"All of them."

He kissed my feet. Rolled down my tights. His warm mouth made my skin feel colder. Lips on ankles, calves, heels. I lay back, pulled my dress over my hips. He stayed there, planting tiny kisses all the way up my inner thigh. Held my waist in both hands.

"She'll be suspicious."

"Yes."

"Don't you care?"

"No."

"What about me? What do you suppose they'll think about me?"

"You're my wife, Beverley."

"Not anymore."

"In spirit. You are in spirit."

I took my knickers off, laughed, and gave them to him. He folded them into a neat square and put them in his pocket.

"Load of rubbish. And you be careful with those."

He ducked his head, ignored me. I sucked in air.

"Easy . . . You said they can wait."

"Sorry," he said, voice muffled. And the rumble of him was like a memory recalled. Then he did the thing I like and I couldn't stop. I put my legs on each shoulder, leaned against the wall, moved my hips, threw myself forward, grabbed his head. Let it all out with a moan that turned into gasped laughter.

"That was good," he said. "Quick."

"Let me do you . . ."

"Wait . . ."

He did it again. I could hear music from the hall, throbbing bass. Lost myself, heard nothing. Jackie would be annoyed, would know, they all would, the elders and cousins I'd never met, the reverend and photographer. He did it again and it happened twice that time. Shuddering, sweet pain. My legs fell. He got up, wiped his mouth. Unbuckled his pants. My legs unsteady as we exchanged places. I kneeled.

"I love you, Beverley Masters."

"Cottrell," I said, and took him in my hand. Patrick laughed.

"God, I'm gonna miss you . . . Oh God . . ." He leaned back, gripped the table.

"That nice?"

"Yes . . ."

I looked up at him.

"I hate you."

"Don't say that . . ."

"I hate you and love you . . ."

"Don't say that, Beverley . . . You don't mean it . . ."

"It's true."

"No one can be me. No one can be us."

"That doesn't matter now, does it?"

I kept on until he began to gasp. I stopped and got up, pulled my dress around my hips, leaned forward on the table. Patrick stood behind me. The first part was every bit as pleasurable as I remembered. The second was never going to be sweet and subtle like the films. Soft focus lighting and light moans. It was hard and brutal, composed of everything between us, a mixture of emotion, necessity, and greed. We were noisy and didn't care. We talked, made idle promises, accusations, teased and joked, nothing like our old way. Patrick kept relentless pace until he thrust hard, four times, fell against me. And in that quick moment I wanted the miracle. I wanted to accept everything and start again, with or without him. I wanted something that was mine, that I could carry in my pocket, but he gave me nothing because nothing was there.

I'd rolled up my tights and pulled down my dress by the time Jackie appeared at the door. Peered through the glass right at me, Father's lodge buddy beside her. Her face, struck with rage. Dragging the elder in a clatter of heels. I fell against the table, hit the rounded corner with my hand, only hurt myself.

"Shit!"

"What's wrong?" Patrick said, adjusting his tie. He hadn't seen a thing.

∽

Q: Why did the young man cross the road?
A: To avoid scaring the lady.

❦

It was strange, coming home to a darkening flat, hoping he'd be there, realizing he wasn't. I hadn't given him keys. I would have some cut. I went into the kitchen, ran the cold tap into a glass. There was a flashing light on the phone dock. I picked up the cordless, dialed 1571.

Patrick's voice had coarsened over the years. He seemed to have gleaned American inflections, and I could hear a child in the background. The clatter of cutlery. The sounds of morning. He was tired, spoke in a neutral tone that was all business, returning my call, the local time, could I call him back or if that was too difficult, could I e-mail. He gave me the address, a new one. Obviously work. Our communication was limited to Christmas cards, the odd birthday if either of us remembered. He hadn't mentioned a child. I felt the resignation, the chore that needed to be done. I held the cordless to my breast, wished I'd erased his message.

When I called Seth, I tried to match my ex-husband's tone. Make it seem as though our last encounter hadn't happened, and my spare room wasn't occupied by the tote bag. I asked him to call or come, whichever was easiest. I tried to push emotion from my voice, but by the time I hung up I knew I'd failed.

In the spare room, I turned on the light. The green bag lay on the carpet, scuffed like sneakers. The room was neat, the single bed made. I opened the bag and rummaged through. Clothes. An open box of condoms, one left. Opened letters. A book, *The Rules of Life*. Newspaper cuttings, some I hadn't seen, detailing what I already knew. Trips to Ghana, the £10,000 reward. The lack of information. The proceedings Seth had told me about that had been simple abstractions until I saw my own words reflected on thin paper. Hope. My need to know. The case had never closed, just grown more perplexing.

I dug deeper, but there was nothing else. If he had any evidence, it wasn't there.

∽

The SCN9A gene is critical for pain perception. It regulates electrical communication between the nerves and the brain. Any variation in the gene can affect our ability to perceive pain. It serves no other function.

∽

That night my kids were subdued, heads bowed, talking amongst themselves. Low energy. It happened. No one outside, they were gathered around tables, on or behind, or sitting with their feet up. Hayley, Vanessa, and Heshima grouped together, listening to tinny music on their phones. Sam on the far side of the class, alone, hands in pockets, looking at the ceiling. Jeff and Chris bunched up, chattering to someone in quick slang, backs toward me, and it was only when I said hello and they parted that I could see who it was. Tall, gray from head to Nikes. Grime Reaper. He looked from beneath the shadow of his hood, gave a stiff nod.

—Y'all right, miss? Jeff asked.

—I am. I see you've brought a friend. Feet off the table, Sam.

They dropped noisily, Sam regarding me with aloof eyes.

—Yeah, miss. Lucien.

—Ah. French.

—Nah, said Grime Reaper. I'm English, innit?

—Well okay, can you pull your hood down, please, we don't allow them in class. How did you all do with the homework?

Grunts, groans. While they were getting seated, Grime Reaper eyeballed me. I ignored him until the clatter of chairs ceased. When he was sure he had my attention, Grime nodded again and dropped the hood, revealing untidy blond hair, green eyes. He eased into the chair between Jeff and Chris, stretched long legs. The girls ignored his show, but Sam was watching my face and Jeff was clearly trying not to laugh. I waited, suppressing my displeasure.

—Anyone? I'd really like to know how it went.

—It was *hard*, miss, Heshima said.

—I don't like writing about myself, Jeff told the room.

—Yeah, we know, said Hayley. Everyone chuckled.

—Well, expressing your inner mind state is a focal part of creative writing. All the greats mine memories. Woolf, Achebe, Cesaire, Greene. Who else do you know so well?

—Yeah, but I don't wanna expose myself, Sam joined in. Like, I don't want everyone to know everyting about me.

—It doesn't have to be everything. You can bend truth, make things up. Leave out bits you don't like.

—And it don't all have to be bad, innit, miss? Vanessa said.

—That's right. You can write a happy memory if you like.

—Man don't have no happy memories, Chris said, smiling at the girls.

—You must have *one!* Heshima said. Vanessa was looking at her notebook.

—Nah man, bare troubles since I was born.

—Okay, take hip-hop, I said, just to bring their attention back. The rapper, the good one, talks of his experience from memory and doesn't glamorize, even though he might not live it now. Do you really think they're out on the streets, hustling drugs and committing acts of violence? No. The famous ones drink in wine bars, have business meetings, eat sushi.

The class erupted in laughter. There was hand slapping, mostly between Jeff, Chris, and Grime. Sam banged the table.

—*Shot*, miss. They shot drugs.

—Whatever, you know I'm not *au fait* with the lingo.

—What? Grime looking at everyone. What'd she say?

I forced a smile in his direction.

—It's French. Like your name. It means I'm not familiar with the words you guys use. Call it international slang, if you like.

He grinned, nodding.

—It's not all bad, Vanessa pressed, face serious. Like in hip-hop, they don't just talk about drugs. They talk parties, relationships, politics . . .

—Lowkey, Chris said, and the room exploded in that strange, almost tribal noise they made, *Brap, brap.* Vocal gunshots. The violence of it scared me, but I continued to smile.

—What's that, a rap style?

More laughter.

—Nah, miss. A rapper, Lowkey. Man's sick, blud, talks about the riots, Blair, alla that.

I grabbed for my notebook, wrote the moniker down. It was nice to know what they were listening to and have an opinion, good or bad. They didn't seem to mind either way.

—Okay, let's have some sharing. Who wants to go first?

Hands waved like a rap concert. I picked Heshima. She read a piece about her younger brother coming home from the hospital, the jealousy she'd felt, her father taking her for ice cream on Portobello Road, her first coffee. It was acutely observed, truthful, and like Heshima, older than her years. She received thunderous applause. Then everyone wanted to read, and we worked our way around the class, each account entirely different from the last. Vanessa wrote about meeting her father for the first time. Hayley, about watching QPR footballers force a rare win. Jeff wrote a lovely piece about the first time he went raving with his dad, infused with an emotion I'd hardly known he possessed. Chris told a story about the day he saw his father beat a man up in a pub fight, which was dark and somehow humorous. Sam wrote about his parents' wedding, ten years after his birth, making the girls melt in their seats and talk of romance.

When the clapping subsided I fished out my journal and read about my father's funeral. Obviously I didn't read the final scene, I just left it when the smell of curry goat wafted about the graveside, but they seemed to like the memory and it tailed into another conversation, and even as they talked I felt we'd already done a good job.

I gave them an exercise, prompted by our discussion. Ghosts. Duppies. Djinns, as Heshima called them. Write a story about a ghost bored with the immensity of time. Begin with any line of their choosing, but if they got stuck they could use, *After I was dead . . .* They groaned as I said that, but when I gave them the usual twenty minutes their heads fell, and they stopped talking after the first five, and then they were hard at it while I read *Cannery Row* for the third time, and I was in tears when Doc hit Mack and Mack let him because he believed he was worthless, wiping my eyes with a finger, hoping the kids wouldn't notice, but they were all writing fiercely, even Grime, and I allowed myself a smile.

They were doing so well I let them go until the end of class, and when I called time they looked up, blinking. Sam and Vanessa kept on; even while I told them we would have to read the work next week. I packed up, waited for my walking companions. Jeff, Chris, and Grime limped by.

—Was that okay? I asked, knowing.

—Yeah, it was live! Grime smiled, which shocked me even though he'd been working. He had one blackened tooth right near the front.

—Be here next week?

—For sure, he said, and then they were off into the night, flipping hoods. I tried not to watch, not to feel anything, but I couldn't stop myself, though I kept my face straight. It felt good.

—Coming, miss?

Hayley and Sam. I rubbed his shoulder.

—Yes, let's go.

❦

Pain and pleasure do not exist beyond oneself. They are entirely in-built, personal sensations.

❦

A tall, broad shadow emerging from a car door. False hope. I strained to see if it was him, guessed it couldn't be. The shadow stepping away from a streetlight, into the darkness of the block. I stopped, grasped Hayley's arm.

—It's a friend. Come by and see me soon.

—All right, she said, squeezing my arm back.

—Sure you're okay, miss?

Sam hadn't moved, even though Hayley was walking.

—I'm fine, honestly. Thanks so much.

He left me then, dragging feet, hands in pockets, a wide space between him and Hayley. I watched them go. Seth came up beside me.

—Evening.

—Seth, how are you?

Kiss, kiss, the slightest of hugs. A lingering hand on my hip. Heat.

—Guardian Angels? he said, nodding at empty space.

—Of sorts, I smiled. They were good tonight.

—Glad to hear it. You look well.

—Do I?

—You always do. But tonight especially.

—Charmer, I said, linking an arm through his. Tell me about your day.

He seemed pleased, slowed his stroll until we were a hair away from being stationary.

—Nothing to tell. Work, home, back to work. Nothing pressing. Got your message and came.

—Thank you.

We moved into the building, the flat. I was still searching for some indication of Wills, a scribbled note or missed call, but there was nothing. I went into the kitchen, poured overproof rum with ice, which I knew Seth liked, trying not to let the absence shatter good feeling. I poured another straight measure for myself and saw the bottle was original dark Trinidadian Plantation rum. A tan label depicting dark men, fields and palm trees, horses, a chattel house. I lifted the bottle, tried to make out faces, but although the men were in profile they were strangely featureless. I felt bad, as though I'd let them down.

I handed Seth the rum. He seemed frightened, took it though. He kept shaking his head, swirling the glass at eye level.

—I shouldn't, really. I'm on duty.

—Shall I put it back?

—No, no, you don't have to. Smells lovely.

—Doesn't it, I said, passing the rum beneath my nose. Like the blood and sweat of past times in a glass.

He shot me a glance, saw I was smiling.

—That's not funny.

—No, it isn't. Sorry.

He sipped, smacked lips.

—Right nice.

—Yes.

—Thought you were annoyed with me. Last time.

—A little. Don't worry, I had no reason. I was angry with the world. Don't you get that way?

—All the time, he said, but it just wasn't so. Seth would never hit me, or make love to me at a funeral, or disappear to America without a backward glance. He might cheat once or twice. Arrest boys who could be my sons. Never lose his temper though. Not that.

—I can't imagine.

—Well, it's true. They're saying I'm a real pain at the station.

—Why?

—Well . . . Seth raised his glass, looked over the rim. It's a sensitive subject. Not for the squeamish.

—Try me.

He shifted, shook the glass. Watched dark liquid.

—So. We get a call to come to the canal, some barge owner's found a body, they say. I've steeled meself because everyone's telling me it's pretty grim, although they say I can handle it. When I get there it's the whole circus, bobbies and flat caps, blue and white tape, forensics on the way. The barge owner's in a state, won't talk to me. I leave him with the PCs, see what we've got.

Seth inhaled, filling his chest, pushed air out. His shoulders fell and the glass rocked in his huge, solid hand. His eyes were red.

—Seth?

—It was a head. A stinking, rotting head in a black plastic bag. A young girl, nineteen they said, from up north. Probably working the streets. Maybe drugs, or got in the middle of two gangs. Domestic or some nutter. Who knows? She's young, that's what got me. Young and pretty. See loads like that, and we always say the same thing. How could it happen, who could do such a thing? But they do. On and on. And that annoys me, sometimes.

—Yes, I whispered.

—So I go back to the station after everything's bagged and done, and I sit and I ask myself that question, and all of a sudden I get this feeling. Like déjà vu, worse. Because I've been there before, I see the faces and files and begin to think, what am I doing? What's changing? Then I think about you, all those years. And I feel so tired, I can't explain—

—Seth, I said, put my glass down, went over. I placed my cold hand on his. The knuckles were flesh-colored rock. He wouldn't look away from his glass.

—Next thing I know, I've leaned back and kicked me desk right over, hard as I could, computer, files, books, phone, the lot. Trashed everything. Then I go to the pub and get steaming pissed.

—That's natural. That's human.

—Not in this job. Not for me.

I rubbed harder, kneading wrists and fingers, crevices and joints.

—I'm sorry, I said. I was terrible to you.

—No. He moved his hand from mine and brought it back, patting my clenched fingers. I deserve what I get. Not you. I don't deserve you. I see it through your eyes, you know. What it looks like. It's not that way, but you wouldn't know. What I have in my heart.

I climbed on the sofa and lay with my head on his lap. Streetlight burst through my window, sunset all night, inner-city beauty. He stroked my hair and drank rum and I wasn't sure how much time passed, but we were there until I grew hypnotized by the rise and fall of his breath, by the soft feel of his fingers against my scalp, and the thoughts began to run. I saw dark stalks of sugarcane, leaves whispering secrets to the breeze. Moist, damp earth, hot and dark. I almost fell asleep until my body jerked, woke me. He was still there, focused on empty space like a troll caught in daylight.

—Don't you have to go back?

—I thought you were sleeping, he said, not even surprised. They'll call. They look out for me. Good blokes they are, the best.

—That's nice, I murmured. And I'll have you know I do see it, Sethin. I do.

—I like it when you say my real name.

—I'm glad. You shouldn't feel bad for me. I have something to tell you. Something good.

—Oh?

I pushed upright, swiping my eyes.

—God. That stuff's too nice. Like a refill?

—I shouldn't. No thanks.

—I want one, I said, and went into the kitchen for the bottle.

When I returned he was straightening his clothes, brushing his pants. The room was shadows and angular shards of light. I liked the way it made things look. Better. I took a huge gulp of rum and sat beside him.

—My son came home.

He frowned, seeing if it was another bad joke. I had to keep the smile from my lips to prove it wasn't, even though he was reminding me of the worn shoe.

—What d'you mean?

I downed my rum, told the story from start to finish, right up until Jackie left. I showed him the tote and we went through Wills's things, the book, the cuttings, torn envelopes, we took them all. We went back to the sofa. I was watching for a reaction but he didn't say anything, and he seemed to have retracted into the persona I hadn't seen in years, had forgotten even existed. Detective Butler. The shell.

—We'll call it in.

I didn't like the way he looked at me. As if I was made of alien rock, a foreign object. Like he'd never seen me, thought I might become glass before his eyes. Waiting for the change.

—I can't . . .

—You have to, Bev. These cases never close . . .

—Not if they don't know, I said quickly. If we say you didn't know. He'll bolt, I know he will, he already asked me not to involve the police.

—Don't you think that's suspicious in itself?

I bit my lip, swallowed protests.

—Yes. Yes, you could see it that way, but I think he wants to protect his abductor. And if you met him . . . If you met him you could tell he isn't like that . . .

—Like what?

—Insincere . . . You'd believe him . . . Please, Seth. Just give me time.

I tried to stare back, match his blankness, but he'd been trained. I shifted in the seat.

—Okay. I won't say anything but I want you to call the minute he does something he shouldn't. And I want you to watch this kid. I don't like what you're telling me. The first thing we should do is arrange a DNA test . . .

—No. Trying to make it sound gentle. No.

—Bev . . .

—Not yet, Seth. I need to earn his trust, and after what happened today, with Jackie and Frank, I'm not sure I have. He'll bolt, Seth, and if that happens, I don't know—

He shushed me then, quiet and tender, as if he didn't want to, held my hand and caressed my fingers. My tear splashed against his broad knuckles and he flinched, tried to let go, but I held on, pulled, moved nearer, pushing my thigh against his. I wrapped an arm around his neck and brought him close. Our lips met. I could taste burnt tobacco, rum like sweet toffee, feel the dryness of his lips against mine, his hesitant tongue. I took my time, touched everywhere. He held back for long moments and I went slow as I dared, twirling his tongue with mine, shallow then deep, until I felt him shudder and moan low in his throat, and I pushed my hand inside his clothes, and he was hot, jerking at my touch, and he fell back against the sofa. I let him go, rolled his earlobe between my teeth. He grabbed the back of my neck, pushed harder.

I stripped him of his jacket, shirt. Got to my feet and took everything off, ran hands over my body. Turned, showed him. He was touching himself, whimpering. I grabbed his wrist and led him into the bedroom.

∽

How much is that doggie in the window?
The one with the waggly tail?
How much is that doggie in the window?
I do hope that doggie's for sale.

❧

In the heat of my intention, of us, I had forgotten. I opened my eyes, saw he was sitting on the edge of my bed. The room was dim so I couldn't see anything but his broad back. He was clothed. I sat up, bracing myself against the headboard I'd clutched, let the sheet fall to my hips. My breasts were not as they had been, but I loved them, knew he did. He didn't move, and that worried me out of the lingering haze of orgasm, the tickle of light sensation, cold air and soft material against my skin.

—Seth?

He turned, and the blank was there again. Only this time it was worse, focused past me. He was holding something in his fingers and I twisted my body, bed-sheet caught around me, to face the headboard and the Post-it note.

Don't sleep with Seth. Ever.

But the Post-it wasn't there. Seth had it.

—Seth . . .

—Don't say anything, he told me, his voice like splintered wood. You don't have to. I understand.

—No, you don't, I didn't mean—

—I understand, he said, and the wood cracked, and he stood, tossed the Post-it on the bed, behind him. Call me if you need me.

—Seth, please . . .

—I can't, he said, and I could hear he was crying, and I was too because I'd made one more mistake, and I would make more, and who could I rely on if not Seth? Ida, my kids maybe, but who with authority, strength?

He walked from the room and I cried with the sheet bunched in my fist, and I didn't have the will to stop him because I had written that note for a reason, I had wanted him to see it, knew he would, and I was a bitch for being so mean when I was fully aware how much he loved me. Because I had been using him since we'd met, and when I'd written that I'd known that whatever happened afterward, I didn't need him. It was my way of unclipping his wings, and such a callous, unfeeling thing to do that I despised myself, even while I was glad it was done.

∽

It was me.
I confess.

∽

After I moved, after I buried my father and before I began to think seriously about the club, after Patrick left and didn't return my messages, even when I tracked him down through the partners and he changed numbers, I fell into a loneliness and depression so dark I forgot I existed, as there were no walls or floors, no ground or sky to remind me. I was unfeeling, numb to the world even when I ventured into it, imprisoned within myself and my grief. I wouldn't answer the phone, or the door, wouldn't dress. The only person who came by was Ida. I'd talk to her through the letter box, wait for her to leave food, quickly open the door and grab the tray, sit in darkness, not eat.

One night I was looking at Caesar, thinking of Malakay and Patrick, a hand deep in the dog's fur, rubbing his neck. I had the photo album open on my thighs and I was crying, once again. I cried every night in those days, before Sue, before the person I became. The album began with all the old pictures. Courtship. Wedding. Birth. Went on to newspaper clippings, pages of them, the dates growing ever wider, Mum's obituary and Dad's, blank white space. Caesar whined. My fingers dug into his neck, just before he growled and moved to the other side of the room. He shot me lowered glances, head on paws, rebuking me. I stared into those eyes for a long time before the dog looked away, but I never stopped watching, never stopped thinking.

I went into the kitchen. His travel cage was in a back cupboard. I wrenched it out, plastic bags and dirty rags falling around me. I opened a tin of his favorite food and placed a small pile at the back of the cage. Of course, Caesar came running. One whiff of meat and dogs always do. As soon as he got inside I slammed the wire door, locked it. Caesar howled, realized he'd been tricked. If I'd had my wits about me I would've done the same to Patrick months ago, I told myself, but in his absence the dog would do just fine.

I took the cage down to my Mini Cooper, threw it on the backseat. Caesar whined and rocked all the way, yelping at me, all rebuke gone, like he was pleading. I drove to the new Sainsbury's, built on the wasteland stuck between the small estate, the rail lines, Kensal Green cemetery, and the Grand Union Canal. I pulled up in the empty parking lot, close to the towpath. The lights made the area look like a landing site. The tar glittered like moonstone and there was no one around, just the occasional car and night bus on Ladbroke Grove.

Beneath the cage, a large sack. I'd bought the Merlin potatoes a few months ago, back when I'd planned to start an allotment and never did, instead giving them to Ida, who made potato dinners for weeks. Varied sizes of home-cooked chips, Bubble and Squeak, shepherd's pie, gnocchi, jacket potatoes, colcannon, fish pie, tumbet, dauphine potatoes, Spanish omelets, and huge plates of sausage and mash arrived at my door every evening. I eventually had to tell her to stop, freeze the dinners, or give them to someone else for the love of God. It was rumored that my family had Irish stock, but I wasn't going to die from overconsumption because of some possible distant relative. Ida, of Irish blood herself, shrugged and said her son would have them. That left me with the unused sack I'd put in my trunk for some reason, probably because there wasn't anywhere else for it.

I took out the cage, laid it down. Caesar was barking to be let out, and I couldn't look at him for fear of losing nerve. I snaked the potato sack over the cage. It fit with room to spare. I tied the end with some rope that had been in the kitchen cupboard since before I moved in, made a thick, tight knot. Another. Caesar was frantic by then, banging against the cage walls, making it scrape across the gravel, and I was glad the parking lot was empty, as he would have been heard, and I would have been arrested. People love dogs, will do anything for them.

I hefted the cage, which was pretty heavy, but I was a tall, strong woman, and if I balanced the brunt of the weight against my hip and walked like a cowboy, it made things easier. Caesar bashed and tried to turn, couldn't because the cage wasn't big enough, but he was a fair-sized collie so his thrashing didn't help. I attempted to drag the cage along the ground but that took so much time I lifted it in two hands, but that was too awkward; I ended up holding the sack away from me so it didn't bump against my leg. That meant I had to put it down every two steps, but I made progress, even if Caesar's yelps were off-putting.

At the canal towpath he was whimpering, a keening high-pitched sound that made my skin crawl. I can still hear it. Water lapped. I wondered if the dog could smell it. There was a faint glow from the barges, but I couldn't hear anyone. I had to be quick, or be seen. I kneeled beside the cage and crooned, told Caesar it was okay, he was Patrick's dog anyway, he'd be happier. I didn't necessarily believe that, but I had to say something. The cage was rocking like a boat on open sea, he was starting to bark again, probably at the sound of my voice, and I didn't even have to do anything, I'd dragged the cage so close all it took was a big rock from Caesar and it went in, bobbing a minute before the sack began to swell like the Wicked Witch of the West, and the barking turned to howls, and the cage went under in an eruption of bubbles, water, and noise.

Thuds and thumps from barges. I got to my feet and ran, fished my keys out of a pocket, dived into the car. I shut the door softly and hid for ten minutes. I cried, but I don't suppose you care.

❦

Pain affects men and women differently. Estrogen and testosterone are partly to blame, although psychology and culture might also account for our variance in the reception of pain signals.

᷍

When I turned up on Sue's doorstep, she took one look and let the door swing open. I walked into her arms, didn't mean to sob, but it happened. She hugged me, stroked my head, and it was everything I needed. A silent tear caught a strand of Sue's hair, and even when she held me at arm's length I could see it winking like a jewel, and I almost forgot why I came, it distracted me so.

They had made good progress. The floorboards were clean and polished, the reception area painted, new art on the walls. She took me into the living room. There was a soft leather sofa, a chaise lounge, a small television, and a floor-to-ceiling bookshelf, neatly stacked. A short ladder on wheels like an old library. There were fresh flowers, pictures of Sue and Howard and her son, and it all looked so perfect. No one was there.

—Would you like a drink? Sue asked.

—Yes, please.

—Gin and tonic?

—Yes, thanks.

—Take a seat, please.

She went over to a small table by the bookshelf. Glasses clinked, the glug of liquid the baritone laughter of a fat, tiny man. The loud fizz of tonic. Dust sheets piled in a corner. A pair of men's slippers at the end of the sofa. The coffee table, a stack of literary magazines.

The glistening spines of books catching sunlight.

—Your timing's impeccable, as usual. Howard's gone to the British Library to write, he says. Probably won't be back until this evening. There's a conference on Tagore.

—Oh. That's nice.

Tanned, smooth legs came closer, stopped.

—There you go.

The glass held before me, the fizz louder. Like a distant audience of thousands. I smiled quickly, took the drink. Sue perched on the edge of the sofa.

—So. What haven't you told me?

We laughed, Sue knowing she was right.

—About Seth, I said. I didn't tell you about our relationship.

Raised eyebrows.

—Seth? Not the boy?

—A little. But more Seth, really.

—Tell me.

I took a deep gulp, emptied the glass. Sue didn't say anything. I was grateful.

—We've been sleeping together. I didn't tell you because it hardly counts.

—How long?

—On and off, years. More off than on. But I didn't want to. Not really, back then. I wanted someone to be with.

—And what happened?

I spun the glass in my hands. Like Seth. How I was feeling must have been vaguely similar to what he'd felt the previous night. I lowered my head.

—You know when you get that sensation? When you relax and don't push?

—You let down your guard.

I looked up, eyes stinging.

—Yes.

—Then what?

—Remember the Post-it notes? You told me to write my feelings. Face them, deal with them.

—Of course. What about them?

—I'd written one. About Seth. How I felt.

Sue frowned, sat back. Took a sip of her gin and tonic, put it down.

—I see. And he noticed it?

—Yes.

The rumble of music, a passing car. Fleeting, gone.

—Should I tell him?

Sue looked confused.

—Tell him?

—How I feel? I don't know what he did, but afterward I felt different, not like I had—

—Are you sure?

Blue eyes, regarding me like Seth. Like the night before. Perhaps the change had happened. Perhaps she was looking at someone else.

—Well, I wouldn't, not unless you're certain. He has a wife?

Nodding, hands twisted in my lap.

—Then you can't. Not unless you're sure.

Head rising and falling, quicker, more resolved, determined to be nice despite all evidence to the contrary.

—You're right. Of course you are.

—And what about the boy?

I shrugged, pushed my lips together. Feigned a smile.

—Did you tell Seth?

—Yes, I did. He wants me to take a DNA test.

I laughed. Sue watched me.

—And what do you want?

—We can, but you know . . . If . . .

—If it's negative.

—Not just that . . . I mean that's bad, but if it's positive . . .

—That could be worse.

I smiled again, really.

—Funny that.

—Yes, Sue said, and reached for her glass. I counted three swallows before she put it down.

—You need to know.

—Yes.

—You need evidence.

—Yes.

—The web is tangled, Beverley. You need to cut free. That's my advice.

—Okay.

—Cut free for your own good.

—I will, I said, and looked her dead in the eye.

∽

Q: Why did the dog cross the road?
A: To avoid the lady.

∽

Crouched in front of the tote bag, extracting items and laying them to one side, by my feet. I'd seen them all the first time, was unsure what I was looking for until

I retrieved the letters. An old one from the unemployment office, another from a phone company, both with his name—*William Emmanuel Price*—and the same mailing address. I wrote it on a piece of paper, typed the postal code into Google Maps. Parson's Green, Fulham. He'd lived in the neighboring borough all those years.

I took the car and drove with Joe Harriott on my stereo. The traffic was bad, and although I took back roads wherever possible, there were still moments when I was stuck behind vehicles, consumed by Harriott's horns, thinking about what I was going to do. I could have called Seth, but I was too proud. I became aware that no one knew where I was going, which went against all of my principles. I couldn't think of anyone to tell. Wills should have been with me, if I'd had any idea of his whereabouts. I had questions, but I was scared of the answers.

My GPS took me to Fulham the long way, I was sure. I passed the subway station at Parson's Green, the green itself, and was directed along a quiet road where the hum of traffic became mute and the people less frequent. A parade of shops, and behind that a small block, the beginnings of what became a full-fledged housing estate. I turned into the block and parked as the final notes of "Jaipur" faded into the soft touch of cymbal. I cut the engine, sat there. Looked at the building in my rearview until I couldn't do it anymore. I closed my eyes, leaned against the headrest.

I was listening to the swing of "Coda" when a knock on my window made me jump. I sat up quickly. A grizzled old man was looking through the window. He closed his fingers into a fist and moved the fist in a circle, as if working an invisible hand drill. I turned down the music, wound down the window.

—You all right, luv?

—Yes, thanks.

—You look a bit sick is all.

—No, I'm fine really. Just tired.

—All right then.

—Thanks for asking.

—Thought I'd better.

—Thanks.

I rolled up the window but he didn't move. I thought he might try and say something else, as he was still peering at me, and after a long time he did open his mouth, seemed to think better, then turned and walked across the lot to the small building taking dolly steps, as though playing a game. I watched him fumble in his pockets for keys, thought about our encounter. I got out my phone and sent a text to Seth, saying what I was doing, and gave him the address too. I may have been foolhardy, but I wasn't entirely stupid.

When I slammed my car door, the old man was gone. I walked as slow as he had, hands by my sides, inexplicably feeling a fizz of blood at my toes. I whistled Harriott, began to scat beneath my breath, conscious nobody should hear me. The keys were in my pocket, digging into my fingertips. The pain was good, it reminded me I was alive and would like to remain that way. There was a thick wooden door before me, hazed glass at the center. An intercom with frosted names written in pen, long illegible. I walked close, glanced around. There were people, no one near enough to see what I was doing. I pushed the buzzer. I bounced on my feet, pushed the keys into the palm of my hand until it hurt. I buzzed again. This time I didn't wait as long, produced the keys, tried the biggest and chunkiest, the one that looked as though it had been gouged at irregular points, inserted. The lock turned.

I pushed inside to find a narrow, quiet staircase. There was a musty smell that could have been the trash chute or the inhabitants, I couldn't tell, and the stairs themselves were concrete, stained brown in places. I didn't want to think about what the liquid had once been. The front doors were sullen, unwelcome, sometimes unpainted, no decorations or attempt to clarify character, just doors. The smell grew stronger and I realized what it was, the collective scent of old people, what I would become. I stopped and thought about that, the passage of time and how quickly it happened, how twenty years had led me in such odd directions, and twenty more could possibly bring me to a home not unlike this place. And the fear came back, but it didn't concern what lay directly before me, behind one of those doors, it concerned what might happen afterward, providing I came through unscathed. The musty smell, the cold staircase, and the building were all part of the nightmare I tried to forget, but I was there, and would return one day for good. Although it was true that I trembled because I was afraid to face the man who had stolen my son, afraid of what I would do as much as what he could do to me, it was also true that there was worse on the horizon. There were places like the building—the smell and the feeling of claustrophobia were so intense I wanted to run from the truth of my advancing age, never look back.

I rested my forehead against the steel banister. The

building would never claim me. I would search for a brighter end. I'd never allow myself to end up that way.

The door, his door, was matte red. Number 7. A brass knocker that once shone. I lifted and let it fall, heard the sound echo down stairs. Pressed my ear against wood and listened. There was no noise. I could have been knocking on the walls of a crypt.

Insert key, turn left, right, watch the door spring open. Push. Hear the creak and curse myself, push harder. A small corridor, a kitchen ahead. Jaundiced grease on cupboards, reproduced paintings on walls, a god-awful stench that rushed me as though trying to escape, pushed me back against the steel banister, a hand on my nose. And I knew what it meant. I guessed what it was, gagged at the thought as much as the smell, but I had to see for myself, otherwise what evidence did I have?

I bunched up my sweater and pressed it against the lower half of my face. Entered and retched again. The smell was putrid, rotten, and yet I kept going, an empty bathroom and toilet to the left, empty kitchen ahead, a door to the right which took me into the living room and the body, head blocked by the expanse of piebald sofa, legs jutting across carpeted floor, slippered feet pointing toward the cloudy yellow ceiling, a smoke gray window of flesh between socks and trousers, thick hair, and just before I turned I thought I saw something run up the trouser leg, something small and dark and stealthy, and that was too much, I had to run back to the staircase, lean over the banister, and throw up over the stairs, listening to the strange musical patter of vomit hitting the ground floor. I did it again, and again, until there was nothing left.

I pulled the front door closed tight, left the block. I was calling Seth before I reached my car.

৵

He sounded off, maybe harassed or distressed, it was difficult to say. Of course, he had good reason, and I didn't push. He said I was a fool for going, fell silent when I told him about the smell, the body. He didn't say much after that, so I had to prompt a response. Eventually he told me he'd talk with someone he trusted, get them to investigate on our behalf and make a search. When he asked if there was anything specific his friend should look out for, I passed on what I knew about the trunk. Seth also told me to stay away from Wills, even though it was clear I would take little notice.

৵

The lights. Those eyes. I can see my spider mother in darkness. She's waiting to see what will happen next, what I might do.

৵

As I pulled into my usual space he was there, sitting by the security door, looking at his feet. I ignored him, parked. When I got out neither of us was smiling. He caught my eye and his head dropped. His fingers were wrapped around a blue plastic bag held between his legs.

—Hey. You came back.

—Yeah.

—Had me worried, I said, hoping that would explain my future behavior, which I couldn't modify I knew. I could feel the difference in my stance, hear it in my voice. The night would be difficult.

—Yeah. Sorry.

—Let's go up.

In the flat, I switched on lights, tried to keep him in front of me. I felt bad about that, but my body wouldn't comply with my guilt. He went straight into the kitchen and I followed, watched him open cupboards. There'd been a familiar smell all the way up the stairs, but I hadn't been sure if it was coming from the flats, the blue plastic bag, or him.

Wills took out plates, cups, knives, and forks. He looked at home moving between cupboards and drawers. He seemed trapped in thought, until he turned.

—Hungry?

—You got takeout?

—Nah. I cooked, innit?

—*You* cooked?

—I can. Smiling. My curry goat's *nice*. You'll see.

—*You* cooked curry goat?

Grinning, taking plastic containers from the blue bag, pushing them into the microwave. *Beep, beep, beep*. He pressed start. The light came on, the machine hummed. Food spun.

—You'll see.

Neither of us said anything. The food turned, smelled divine. Wills removed two Styrofoam cups from the bag, took the lids off both, and poured them into tall glasses. He gave me one.

—Taste this.

I took a sip, widened my eyes.

—You squeezed golden apple?

—Nah. Smiling wider. Bought. Thought you'd like it.

—That's very thoughtful, Wills. Thank you.

—That's okay.

A long beep. Wills extracted the containers, opened them. Steam rushed toward the ceiling, and I smelled it properly, tasted bile. He spooned meat and rice onto the plates with great care, presented the first with his eyes down. I took it, scanned the plate without being obvious. There was allspice in the curry, gunga peas in the rice.

—Well, you obviously know what you're doing.

—Thanks.

I took my plate and juice into the living room. After a while, Wills joined me. He took his seat, began praying under his breath, ate. He looked cleaner, clothes and skin. When he'd come close I'd smelled soap, maybe deodorant. His hair was less matted, eyes clearer. He'd been sleeping well. I tasted the food. Gorgeous.

—So, you've been at Vicky's?

—Yeah.

Eyes on plate, loading spoon with knife.

—How's her boyfriend?

—Husband . . . Wills saw me start. He's gone to Birmingham to visit family. Only reason I could stay, innit?

—Husband?

—Yeah.

—That must be difficult. For everyone.

—It is.

I wanted to ask if anything other than simple friendship was going on. I wasn't sure if I could. I couldn't decide whether it would be my place even if we had spent our lives together. I found myself staring at him, thinking about time again, all that had passed and all there was to come, exactly how much either of us knew about the other.

In silence, Wills's spoon gathered pace. I remembered my own plate, ducked my head. Thought I saw something move between the chunks of meat, probed with my fork. Lifted and turned. There was nothing but allspice berries, black like the eyes of fried fish, but I was still spooked, still saw the stiff legs of the man. My stomach rolled. I picked through my food, selected a piece of meat, rice, put the fork in my mouth. Took a dry swallow. It went down hard, like a lump of solid matter in my throat, even though it tasted good.

—This is lovely, by the way.

—Thanks.

—Tastes like the real thing. Not mutton or lamb.

—Cos it is. They got a cool butcher's down Vicky's way, English brer, sells halal. Good meat, not a lot of bone or fat, nice cuts.

—Your grandfather used to love curry goat.

—For real?

Wills stopped chewing, was regarding me. Allspice eyes, blank like my spider mother.

—Yes. At his funeral, as we were burying him, the smell of curry was everywhere. It smelled like this.

—Don't lie . . .

—Ask Jackie and Frank. He made the best curry goat I'd ever tasted.

—That's nuts, Wills said, and went back to his plate.

—I wanted to ask you something, actually.

—Go on, Wills said.

—Are you Muslim or Christian? I see you pray but I can't tell. You speak so quietly.

He was nodding.

—Buddhist.

—Oh.

—People never know what to say.

I smiled, ate. He waited for me to swallow.

—It's a surprise. But I happen to think if I was religious, that would be the one I'd choose. Or Jain.

—Yeah. I almost chose that, but no one knew what it meant.

He laughed, and I laughed with him until I remembered. The smell. That flat. The stiff legs. And my smile died, my lips flatlined.

—It's good to be part of something. To feel like you belong, I said, watching him.

—Best feeling in the world.

—Yes. I said. It is.

❦

Behçet's disease, or Behçet's syndrome, is a condition that causes wide-ranging symptoms, including mouth ulcers, genital ulcers, and eye inflammation. It is rare in the UK, at only two thousand sufferers. Symptoms are caused by inflammation in the small blood vessels, though it's not clear why they become inflamed. At present, there is no cure, although the pain can be treated. Many sufferers believe their symptoms are psychosomatic.

❧

Television as the flat grew dark, lights and small talk. There was so much I wanted to ask, so much I wanted to impart, but it all seemed irrelevant or unsayable, not worth the energy. We sat in silence through the news, the evening shows, and before I knew it, the news at ten, and I began to yawn. Long day. Wills hadn't moved, so I took his plate and glass and washed off the residue, put them into the dishwasher. I was trying to equate the boy with the corpse of the man, trying to imagine the scenario that might have led to his demise, to put Wills in the picture. And as much as I did, I couldn't see it. That blind spot scared me most, it was like peering into a dark room, knowing my nightmare fantasies were ridiculous, fearing the unknown. The truth was, I didn't know how the man had died. He had quite possibly been there for weeks. And although my mind's eye wouldn't let me see Wills, I was fully aware that this could be my greatest failing. The more I tried to relax and not think about it, the worse I felt. Even the brash, intrusive light of the kitchen only served to highlight the dark of the living room, and when I went to the door and looked, I couldn't see him.

I turned off the kitchen light, went further. Wills was immobile in front of the TV, feet outstretched.

—I think I'm going to bed.

—Oh. Okay, cool.

—Thanks for dinner.

—Least I can do, innit?

—Goodnight, Wills.

—'Night.

So much between us, so much unsaid. I went into my bedroom and quietly slid the lock closed. I wanted to push something in front of the door, decided against it. I stood there, looking at the door, hoping I hadn't made a mistake I would regret, like the Post-it notes. The phone rang. I sprawled on the bed, answered.

—Hello?

—Bev. Seth.

—Ah. I was just thinking about you.

—Were you now?

—Yes. I was. How are you?

—Good, good. Better.

Shame arced through me, and my eyes closed.

—That's a relief.

—How are things with you?

—Okay. I lowered my voice. He's back.

—Right. A rumble of breath against my ear. I imagined I could feel it, could smell rum and cigarette. I suppose you'll want to know what they found.

—I suppose.

Mouth open, bracing myself.

—It's early days, and they'll need to do an autopsy before they can determine COD . . .

—What?

—Cause of death.

—Oh. Of course. Silly.

—The paramedics usually make an assessment, and that's what we go by until postmortem.

—Makes sense.

—So, they suspect cause of death to be a stroke or heart attack, but I'm stressing they're never sure . . .

—I understand . . .

—They just say these things and my colleague reports them, that's all I'm saying . . .

—What else did they find?

Big breath. I was frowning.

—Ah, Bev.

—What is it, Seth?

—Can't fool you.

—Please, Seth, I whispered, looking at the door. Please.

—All right. He had a nasty bump on his head. Not enough to actually kill him, but it must have bloody hurt. What the autopsy will have to try and determine is when it happened.

—But it could have been the fall, right?

—He was quite old. He could have had the attack, fallen over, and bumped his head on the sofa. Or—

—He could have been hit and had the attack afterward. Caused by the blow.

—That's right.

—Shit.

I heard movement. Footsteps outside my door. I lowered my head until my lips brushed the duvet.

—Yes.

—God. How awful.

—We found things too.

—Like?

—He was ex-police.

I couldn't speak, even think.

—A long time ago, not high ranking, but we found papers. A constable. PC Edward Price.

—My God.

—I'm truly sorry, Bev.

—I know, I said, and I felt a rush of empathy like

never before. I wanted him to come over and hold me, make love to me, bring back what I'd felt. I gritted my teeth, only realized when the molars scraped against each other. What else?

—We found the trunk. It had news clippings and baby clothes. A great deal about you. We're pretty sure it was him, Beverley. We think he was the one.

The bed was rocking. It twisted and turned beneath me and I pushed my body against the mattress, holding the corner with my free hand, wanting Seth beneath me, afraid to say the words. The room spun. I closed my eyes until I heard a clang outside my door. I saw something in my own darkness, eight lights in paired rows. My eyes shot open. I could taste curry goat.

—Beverley?

—Yes, I'm here, I said, and heard how tiny my voice was, how frail. Are you sure?

—Eighty percent. It happens a lot, someone who slipped the net dies and the whole bloody thing comes out. Or he could be some random nutter who took a shine to your case, obsessed. Never can tell. Obviously I can't do anything without your say so, but we'll know for sure when we launch the full investigation.

—Thank you. I appreciate everything, Seth.

—That's all fine and dandy, but you're living with a potential threat.

—I know. I need time.

—It's dangerous, Bev. You don't know who he is.

—He's my son.

—That's not what I meant. And, forgive me, but you're not even sure of that.

—Fair enough.

Movement. A thump against the adjoining wall. He was in the spare room, bedding down. Or trying to overhear my conversation.

—Seth, I'm going to go. He's right here, in the next room.

—Call me tomorrow.

—Yes.

—Make sure, Bev. I want you checking in a minimum of three times a day. Even by text.

—I will. I promise.

—And if he even sniffs at you wrong, I'll let the whole world know. You know that, don't you?

—Of course.

Seth sighed.

—Okay, love. Speak tomorrow.

—Goodnight. Thanks again.

—No worries, he said, and rang off.

I lay the phone on my bed, rolled over. I stayed that way until I got up and dragged my chest of drawers in front of my bedroom door. I undressed and went to bed. I guessed I might sleep badly, and I was right.

᷍

My eyes grow accustomed to darkness. I begin to make out solid forms, some inanimate, others not. I cannot see. What I mean is I do not want to. I wish myself blind, know how awful a thing that is, can't help feeling it's what I want. I get up and tiptoe into the bathroom, lest I make a sound that is detected. I take a towel from the rack, the thickest, bring it to the living room. I don't know why I haven't done this earlier. Shock, maybe, or simple foolishness. I tie it as tight as I can, over and over, ignore the gasps, ignore the pain, ignore everything.

∽

Staring at my ceiling, alert to every sound. As a result, I slept in late. There were noises from the kitchen at some point I couldn't remember later, and I sat up, grateful for the chest of drawers barrier, fell back into sleep. My dreams were rapid and nonsensical, one merging into another, and when I woke I couldn't recall them. Light shone from the window, directly into my eyes. I crawled from the bed, hunched over. My bedside clock said eleven thirty. When I stood prone and listened, I couldn't hear anything.

I dragged away the chest of drawers and walked out, tentative. The living room was empty, and the kitchen, and the bathroom. He'd gone. I found a note on the kitchen counter. *Gone to Vicky's, Love W.* I was relieved, ashamed. I made cereal and sat before the blank TV.

After a while I washed and dressed, trying to work out a reason. The only one I could think of was that I wouldn't like Wills to see me in my dressing gown late in the afternoon. He might question my sanity. He had enough to go on. I tried to pick a book from my shelf, one I hadn't read, but I couldn't find my way into the narrative. I wrote in this journal. It was difficult to get started, my thoughts scattered, sentences halting, but then something happened and I wrote without stopping or thinking for a long time, and when I looked up from the page it was filled with my scrawled handwriting. I turned back a few pages. The words scared me. Hundreds, marching. Dark patterns like a trail, a black spider's web. I shook my hand and it cramped in the flesh between my thumb and first finger. I threw down the pen, rolled my head, heard my neck creak. I checked the time. 14:33.

After a quick lunch, I picked up my battered leather diary. Held it in one hand, the cordless in the other. I tried to dial with my thumb but that was awkward and I had to put the diary on the table. The phone rang forever, long tones that sounded gruff, belligerent, like a complaint. I was about to hang up when there was a click, and the sound changed. I could hear soft music, the chatter of a radio.

—Hello?

A child, high voice tethered to excitement.

—Hello, darling. How are you?

—*Goo-ood* . . .

Stretching the word like bubble gum.

—That's wonderful. You're a good boy. And how old are you?

—Uh . . .

I waited, eyebrows raised.

—Go on, tell me. How old?

—Uh . . .

I waited longer, until it was clear he either didn't know, or wasn't going to tell me.

—That's okay, baby. That's okay. Could I speak with Daddy, please?

Light breath, silence.

—Hello? Are you there?

The rattle of exhalation, the whistle as air met teeth. I closed my eyes, too late to catch tears. I was angry with myself. Always crying. I wasn't like that before.

Another voice, distant.

—Kumari, who's on the phone?

No reply.

—Go and get Mummy, baby, let me speak with Mummy.

—Kumari, honey, will you pass the phone! No one wants to listen to you all blowin down the line . . .

The voice came closer. There was a squeal, a series of loud bumps.

—Goodbye, baby, I whispered, his cries fading.

—Hello, can I help?

Brisk, bright, all business.

—Yes. You can. This is Beverley. How are you?

—Oh.

Ice, crackling and quick, turning what was warm and open into a vast desert, flat, cold, empty. I was rubbing my head, thrown, nervous.

—He seems very bright. Kumari, is it?

I paused for a reply, realized there wasn't one. Kumari wailed in the background.

—We've not spoken, really.

—No.

—It's a shame. I was hoping we could be friends.

—Oh, *really?*

It wasn't going to work. I wasn't even sure why I was trying, if I would have felt differently had I been in her place.

—Is Patrick there at all? I've been trying to call and I left a message—

—I know. He called back.

—Yes. And I'm returning the call.

—He won't be home until this evening. He's at work.

—Oh . . . So, could you tell him I rang?

—Yeah, sure.

I didn't believe her for a minute. I wouldn't have told.

—Look, Rachelle, I just want to . . . Well, I don't know . . .

She said nothing, left Kumari catching his breath not far from her. Hiccupping words. Coming to the end of tears. Soon he'd begin to play again, forget. Only later transgressions would form scars he might remember. Only time would mark him.

—I wanted to let you know that I wish you well. All of you. I wish you all the best in the world. You have my blessing. Always have.

—I know what you did, Rachelle hissed.

—I'm sorry?

—I know what you did, at your own father's funeral. You don't respect him and you certainly don't respect me. Stay away. Do you hear?

—Okay, I whispered. Okay.

—Stay away from us. I mean that.

Click. I put the cordless down.

❦

Books I would like to read:

- *War and Peace*, Leo Tolstoy
- *The African Trilogy*, Chinua Achebe
- *The Lord of the Rings*, J.R.R. Tolkien
- The Bible

❧

There was nothing else to do but wait. Wills left the house each morning, presumably to take care of Rae and spend time with Vicky while her husband was at work. I sat indoors, alone. In the evenings he would come back. One of us would cook. We'd eat and talk of inconsequential things: soap plotlines, the latest news, Vicky's daughter. Wills had people to care for, who in turned cared for him. I watched daytime TV and wandered local parks by myself.

Occasionally I would see Ida, although things were not the same. It was difficult to tell what had happened, but she seemed reserved too, had retracted like Seth, to a safer distance maybe, beyond the place where any fallout might cause harm. It was clear she didn't approve. I'd known Ida a long time, had seen that wrinkle of pursed lips in the shops when a sales assistant got on her nerves, or on the bus when someone sat too close, or when she spoke about the estate kids. Now, for the first time, it was directed at me. When I bumped into her on our landing she was quiet, watchful. She didn't have much to say.

I decided to confront her. One morning when Wills had left for Earl's Court and I was sitting in the house alone, I got up, retrieved a green paper bag from the kitchen, slipped on house shoes, and headed down the landing. I knocked. She opened up right away, as if she'd been waiting. Her expression was blank, fixed as soon as she saw me.

—Hello, love.

—Hey, Ida. How's it going?

—All right.

—Haven't seen you for a while. Was worried.

I laughed, stopped. Ida's lips were thin, hardly noticeable.

—Yeah, well, you've got company. Didn't want to intrude.

—Oh, Ida. That's silly. You're welcome anytime, you know that.

—I know. It's me, love. Don't want to get in the way. Third wheel and all.

Her shoulders looked thin. I noticed she had a small blanket wrapped around herself. Her skin was pale. I could see arteries, blue rivers mapping the landscape of her neck.

—Did Graham come?

—Yes. Last week.

—Oh. Why didn't he come around, say hi?

—Flying visit.

—Oh. I looked at my feet. The frayed, curled mat said WELCOME. The letters were faded. I brought you this.

Giving her the bag, watching her face. She took it, untied the bright red ribbon, and opened up. Dug a hand inside and retrieved thick, uneven bulk.

—Chocolate?

—Ninety percent raw, organic. You can use it in cakes.

—Thanks, love. Appreciate it.

I couldn't tell from her face. It was a smooth sheen, lifeless.

—Are you all right, Ida?

—I'm fine. Absolutely fine. I'll go down to Cornwall in a bit, see my son. I'm all right.

My eyes began to prickle. Ida noticed, looked down. I gulped my voice back into my throat.

—Come by and see us anyway.

—You're busy, love, you and your young fella. I'm all right.

—But Ida, that's not—

—I'm all right, she said, and retreated behind the door, and smiled, false as dentures. See you before I go?

—Sure.

—All right, she said, and closed the door.

I walked down the landing, replaying what had been said. Then it hit me—*third wheel* and *your young fella*—and I knew just what she meant. I couldn't correct her because I didn't want her to know the truth. It was difficult to say what hurt worse, her sick assumption or the fact that she hadn't let me into her house for the first time in all the years I'd known her.

I didn't cry. My eyes burned and shame caused my gut to contort, but no tears fell.

At the club, I went through the motions of imparting information, wisdom, and energy, but I could feel something had transpired, and whether they were responding to it, or were just that way themselves, was hard to tell. There was weight around my eyes, like the urge to sleep but more forceful, and my irritation was ever present, snatching at the kids, never quite grasping, though it kept trying. My kids were mute, cautious, eying me like a bad parent, someone to be afraid of, even Grime Reaper and Jeff, who kept their heads down and got on with work, cracked little jokes. I looked at Sam every so often, but he wouldn't meet my eye. Hayley, Vanessa, Chris, and Heshima—no one dared.

While they did an exercise, I went to the bathroom. I washed my hands and looked in the mirror and saw sacks beneath my eyes. I couldn't tell whether they were red-tinged or if the lighting made them that way. I didn't look good. My skin was pale. I radiated stress.

I returned to class fully aware what they were seeing, which didn't make my performance any better. We mentally limped through the final minutes to the end of the session. I assigned homework, let the kids go. Sam and Hayley walked me, but it felt more perfunctory than ever, and when I waved them goodbye I found myself wishing they would never walk me again. From the ground floor, in the parking area, I looked up at my flat. I didn't want to be there either.

∾

Rolling dark clouds, somber ocean. Vast, eternal, as far as I could tell, neck craned upward, looking for a break. I shaded my eyes, too bright, summer in all but deed. The wind blew around my knees, cooled them. I pulled up my socks.

"What are you doing?"

She was squinting, eyebrows lowered, trying to raise them. I caught an image of how I must have appeared: head thrown back, mouth open, scanning clouds as though balancing a sword on my nose. I relaxed, shrugged.

"Nothing."

We stood a meter apart, not near enough, closer than other girls. They were scattered like marbles, rolling into adult embraces, into cars, holding tiny dogs high, dancing to pop blasting from car speakers with infant siblings. Radio One. I looked behind us. The principal, waving in the general direction of the parking lot, flowing black robes. Yards away, on the other side of the road, I caught sight of the Mercedes, sleek and silver, a languid basking shark. I held Maise's hand.

"You'll call?"

"Of course," I smiled. "You can come and stay in London."

"I'd like that," she said, and squeezed my hand. She peered over my shoulder.

"I think your dad's here."

"Really?" Quick glance, as though I hadn't seen him. "How did you know?"

Maise wrinkled her nose. It had taken months to learn that was how she smiled. I grinned, we hugged. My father was the only other person of color in sight.

"You go. I'll ring next week."

"Sure? I don't mind waiting."

"It's okay. They'll be here."

Looking over gathered people, trying not to focus on one spot.

"All right, Maise. Speak soon."

I walked to the Mercedes, trying not to be aware, not to notice the stares of adults and children, trying to keep my head straight. Obviously I failed. I could feel the tickle of my skirt against the backs of my knees, had to bend to pull my socks up. Dad was watching. Window rolled down, playing reggae. Though it was low, I still looked over my shoulder.

"Hello, pudding."

"Hi, Daddy."

I leaned through the window, kissed his cheek. We hugged.

"Ah," he said. "That's better."

I went around the other side, got in.

"Where's Mum?"

"Jackie has a recital."

"Oh." I studied my gleaming knees.

"Does your friend need a lift?"

"Oh no, she's okay. Her mum and dad are always late."

"Sure?"

"Positive," I glowered. "Really."

Dad nodded, started the car. A lazy growl of power, the rumble beneath my thighs. I leaned back, closed my eyes, and was pushed into my seat. Dad always liked to drive fast.

We made small talk about school, my classes and tutors, some prefect I couldn't stand, until we hit the motorway. Dad turned up the music. I recognized Dennis Brown, didn't know the song. He was crooning his heart out and Dad was singing along. I watched the flash of green alongside us, passing cars. I felt my stiff jutting lip, my dark clouds. I began to notice something, every thousand yards or so, wasn't sure what until I leaned closer to my widow, unclipped my belt. Thick, dusty fur. Bodies curled like commas. The glitter of sunlight on blood. Road kill. I counted fifteen before I felt sick.

"Beverley?"

I rolled on my back, face clenched, a hand on my belly.

"Pudding, you okay?"

I nodded, mouth closed. "Feel a bit sick."

"Want me to pull over?"

I shook my head slow.

"Well, let me know, okay? And fasten your belt."

Dad was shooting me quick glances. Road, me, road, me. He paid more attention to the road. I knew that was right, but it still annoyed me. He turned the music down. I did as he asked.

"I was actually wondering if you were okay in a more . . . general sense . . ."

I wished he'd turn the music back up. Blast it, drown words.

"Yes, Daddy." I focused on taillights, constellation windscreen bugs.

"Well?"

I dug in my pockets, couldn't find any, dug in the glove compartment. He was patient. The gum was in the little space behind the handbrake. I retrieved the pack, offered, took one, and chewed. Felt pain as my taste buds exploded. Winced.

"Daddy, are we poor?"

My father didn't look at me, kept his eyes on the road.

"I only ask because Clarissa Martin always goes on about the lower classes whenever I'm in the room, and I swear it's because in Cervinia they were bragging about how much they had to spend, and when they asked me I told them ten pounds, and they all laughed, and said that was ludicrous, and how they could never live on so little, and when they asked Maise even she said forty, and that was nothing to them but it was still better. And Izzy's mother bought her a car for her sixteenth and she's giving her lessons over the holidays, and you know, I *hate* being poor."

Dad said nothing. He opened his mouth, gripped the steering wheel, closed his mouth. Dennis wailed.

"Do you feel poor?"

I threw my head back, heard the thud. Too loud.

"Well, *duh!*"

I lifted my head. Dad was looking at the road. I felt bad because I could sense something trapped in the car. I didn't know what, but it rips at me now, those infantile emotions. I wanted him to look at me, couldn't figure out how to make him. I tried to watch the road, see what he saw. The white line, cat's eyes. The Mercedes eating each and every one like Pac Man. The buildings, blue signs.

"Hungry?"

"Yes, Daddy."

He pulled into the service station. We locked up, went inside. We stood in line and purchased our food, chips and some form of processed meat, walked back toward the exit. I was chewing on chips when I realized Dad wasn't there. He'd stopped behind me. He inclined his head to the right.

"Come nuh."

A minimart, scaled-down shelves to match the staff, who seemed subdued and inert, on standby. Dad led me down the aisle by the hand until we reached a rusty, humming fridge. I clasped my arms around myself like the game we'd played when we first got to school, pretending to kiss boys after lights-out. Dad reached into the fridge, wrapped massive fingers around a margarine tub.

"See this?"

"Yes, Daddy."

"This is made from edible fat. To make edible fat, there's a process which involves refining oil."

"Okay."

I looked at my Clarks. The tone of my father's voice was deadly serious, his posture was serious, and his expression was so serious I hardly recognized him. Dad touched my cheek, lightly.

"I devised that process." He ducked his head, looked into my eyes. Lifted my chin. "I'm not scolding you."

"I know, Daddy." I gulped, not feeling better, not understanding.

"Good. This is why I work hard, why you, your mother, and sister, and any children either of you have, will want for nothing. This is our foundation, right here. Can you hold it, see what it feels like?"

He gave me the tub. I hefted it in my hands. He was looking at me with such intent I didn't want to let him down. The margarine felt cold, rock solid. It could easily hurt someone.

"It's heavy," I said. "Small and heavy." I gave back the tub.

"Little but talawa," Dad grinned, and rubbed my head.

❧

So quiet, like the still of cane or the bush when an eagle soars. Like London streets in that final seam between night and approaching dawn. The days passed and time rolled and I studied Wills for signs. Texted Seth and heard nothing. Saw the blank of Ida's closed door. Saw my silent phone and assumed Rachelle hadn't passed on my message. Some nights I dreamed of roaring fire, rows of eyes. Of wooden legs in the living room, a putrid body swelling until it burst, the wriggle of insects. The smell. I would wake and see him in my house and be afraid. When I was alone, on my sofa, I caught a low rumble on the edge of my hearing, a constant sound just beyond imperceptible, and I knew something was coming. For me, for us.

Sunshine, colors, the constant sound engulfed by a new noise. Movement and laughter, random tears. Grimy faces, toothless smiles, waddling footsteps, and, of course, piercing screams from every angle. Bumps, shouts of triumph. Dodging tiny bodies to avoid self-ish progress. It had been an age since I'd visited the park without passing by those sacred places, but I had a need, there was a reason, and I plastered a grin across my face that would not be shifted, would not reveal, and Wills seemed the same, running behind Rae as she shot toward rope-climbing frames, up and up like Spider-Girl, leaving me on a bench, hands clasped, smiling in all directions, beside Vicky.

She was huddled against the cold, the wind, even though the sun was visible, the sky blue. Hands in pockets, neck buried in her shoulders like a young bird. Her teeth chattered. I slid closer.

—Cheer up. Thought you'd be used to it by now.

—God, man, never. An imagine this is spring. A few months ago it was all about one o'clock club, truss. I ain able for being out here when it's gray and rainy and windy like them hardnut nannies.

—Nannies?

—Yeah, poor tings. Tarquin wants to play on the

ship, or the wooden house, so they gotta come out rain, sleet, or snow. Don't be fooled, she said, seeing my shock. None ah them people ain their parents. All them Asians. An even the white ones, listen close and they ain from London. Lithuanian, Sardinian, Russian, Polish . . . We talk sometimes and they say the kids are fine when they're young, it's just when their older. Proper spoilt! Orderin them around like adults. Nuts.

—Wow.

—It is South Ken, Vicky said. She squinted into the distance, dug in her pockets and retrieved a pack of cigarettes. She lit up, taking quick puffs. Oh, sorry. Want one?

—No thanks. I gave up.

—Good deal, she said. She blew rings, good ones. Is it funny? Like, weird?

—What's that?

—Being here. With him.

I squirmed on the bench, gaps against my thighs.

—A little . . . Although, to be honest, the kids make it worse. It's like being bombarded . . .

—I'm sorry, Vicky said. We could have gone somewhere else. I did say . . .

—It's fine. I can't run forever. It's been long enough.

—I hear that. She threw the cigarette underfoot, stomped it. There must have been at least half left. She stood up. Yes, I see you! Look at you! Well done! Can you go higher? Can you go higher, baby? Brave girl! She sat back down, pushed hands into pockets. God. Cuttin, man.

—And how are you two?

She gave me a sidelong glance.

—*This* feels funny. Talkin about us.

—You don't have to.

—Yeah, well, I started it, she laughed. I smiled back, meant it. We're good. I mean, as good as we can be. Daryl's eased up since Wills moved out, which makes things better. For Rae especially. We're getting on better as well, me an Wills.

—That's good.

—I'm gonna help with his college applications, when he gets them. I'm gonna go too, part time, evening classes.

—Brilliant.

—Gonna do accountin an Spanish. I'm good at both.

—Very good skills.

—We don't sleep together, you know, she said, head straight, watching Rae maybe. Not while Patrick's home. Just so you know. Wills is real good. He gets it.

—A gentleman?

—Oh, totally. We've hardly done it in all these years.

—That's love.

—You think so?

I nodded once, stiff.

—I think so.

I touched her shoulder and she grinned.

—What was he like before? When he lived with Eddie, or in the hostel?

—How d'you mean?

—Tell me about Wills. He's very quiet.

—Truss, Vicky said, and laughed again.

—So what was he like? Anything would be a massive help.

Vicky's eyes formed black darts.

—He was less talkative. Oh yeah, really. One of the quietest kids in our year. He used to hang with all the mans dem but not really, know what I mean? Always on one side, didn't get involved. But when tings happened he would do tings.

—I know a few like that.

—Nuff girls fancied him. The ones that didn't favor dem loud youts.

—Like you.

She grinned wider.

—Like me. And then he got into the black shit, cos Eddie was into it, I reckon, no one else. Panthers an Malcolm an all that. Started chatting Egypt pyramids shit an all dem shotta youts jus drifted, except coupla his close boys. I used to catch Wills at the library dem times. All up until it closed.

—That was good though, right?

She wriggled her shoulders, trying to loosen a kink.

—If you don't overdose. Trouble with black shit is once you got the knowledge you gotta deal wiv the fact you can't leave. You're in the belly ah the beast an it's *hot*. Babylondon. Home and hell.

—It's hard.

—Sure is. Vicky sat on her hands. He used to put on events, like rap and poetry nights, positive stuff. He used to perform his own music.

—Was he good?

Vicky scrunched up her face like she'd eaten something sour.

—No.

We laughed.

—Then I dunno, it was like he mussa start notice certain things an couldn't stop. Couldn't un-notice. That's what happened. First the teachers, then the shottas.

—What do you mean?

She saw me then, in one quick moment; I mean, she saw the shine of my eyes, and she swiveled again, black darts on her child.

—You said you was gonna ask him all that.

—I am.

—So why you askin me?

Spat half in my direction, half at gravel.

—What do you want me to do? Step in his face and ask why he was expelled? What happened in that house?

—Yes.

—Well, it's a bit more complex than that. Last time someone asked Wills a question he disappeared to your place. Next time he might go farther.

—He won't.

—So you say.

Vicky glared, dug in her pockets.

—Make me wanna cigarette, man, she muttered.

I let her open the pack, light. We looked over the playground at the same time. Rae was on the swings, Wills pushing.

—What happened at school? With the teacher and his friends?

Smoke rushed in my direction, doubled back as though it had changed its mind. More followed.

—Vicky, come on. Help me out. I live with him.

—I did.

—You had the benefit of making an informed choice.

Speaking toward the playhouse and rectangle of sand pit.

—I have a husband an daughter. You think I'd let him in the house if he was dangerous?

I thought about that, forced myself to take time. I was losing patience, biting my tongue so I wouldn't snap, weighting my tone with false lightness, like my smile.

—Vicky. Is he violent? Did he hurt someone at school? That's all I want to know.

She crossed her legs, made the top one bounce.

—That's why he was expelled, wasn't it? He got into a fight?

She rose in a blast of smoke and movement, walking across the tarmac before I could reach out or say anything, across balding grass and into the main playground area, its soft green floor and bouncy bikes shaped like animals.

—Rae, babe, you got five minutes an it's time to go, Uncle Wills must be proper tired, you little devil . . .

I pulled my coat tighter, watched them laugh.

∽

Things to do:

- Renew cinema membership
- Find clip for rubber gloves
- Finish watching *Charulata*
- Buy rum
- Take jeans back to TK Maxx
- Nose thing
- Be kind, for everyone is fighting a great battle

∽

Fluorescent light made my head pound, a soft and resounding drum, though I pushed on, perhaps feeling I was losing touch, perhaps fighting tiredness. I don't know, I can't remember. They looked at me, my kids, spread across the class in various states of lounged behavior, only Vanessa and Heshima alert, although I could see the others were trying, at least as much as I was. And when I thought how off I'd been over the last few weeks, I began to feel bad, as it was quite late, and they were still there, had been for months. Grime Reaper had come every week since the first, and that made me smile, thinking of their loyalty and the fact that I'd been so caught up in Wills I'd missed seeing I was loved, had always been. It's strange the things you notice just before it all happens, and I'm not sure even now whether that's hindsight or I actually had the thought, the only thing I remember is smiling, them smiling back, tired, as I recited the week's homework.

We left the building. That night it seemed as though Chris and Jeff and Grime had managed to get through to Heshima and Vanessa, telling jokes, making them smile at the sidewalk and join them, tugging invisibly in the opposite direction of home, and so they came with me and Sam and Hayley, saying something about George's Fish and Chips. The group seemed to have come together and the night was warm, everybody walking side by side, bumping each other, not saying sorry, just muttering, or holding a shoulder to steady themselves, push upright, me in the middle surrounded by kids. And it felt good. I can't deny it felt like family, in a way I'd long forgotten. When I looked up at the multiple eyes of the estate and saw reflected sodium lights I didn't feel afraid, I just closed my eyes, let jostling bodies guide me.

Conversations formed, the group began to separate. Jeff and Chris slowing. Vanessa and Heshima hanging back. Sam and Hayley on either side of the white line, the empty road. Somehow I found myself walking next to Grime, who was a head taller than me, talking about nothing, music mainly, him speaking rapidly about the art of rhyme, how much he'd realized it owed to the art of literature, and how he listened to what rappers were saying more already, not just the music, and saw most of them "chat breeze," as he put it, and how he'd decided to pen songs himself, although he was just beginning, had a way to go, but he'd always been good with words.

I suggested books—Chester Himes, Donald Goines, Iceberg Slim—even though I'd found them all hard going, told the boy he was a natural storyteller; if he'd only read more he could easily write prose. I witnessed the light in his eyes when I said it, the pride. I felt good, re-energized. We turned into my cul-de-sac, slowed a little so we could finish what we'd been saying.

Shouts, noise, a banging door. Voices. I was moving, leaving Grime, head craned toward my landing, hearing the clatter of my footsteps against concrete. Hearing the voices of my kids, nothing they were saying. Up on my floor, more voices, raised and shrill, and I knew them even though they were joined in anger, combined to create a shrill song, all high octaves. I could see them, quick flashes, Jackie pointing, shouting something. I saw Frank beside her, and Wills, he was holding something in their direction, and they were backing away, shrieking. Cold ran through me as though I'd been doused.

A quick look at my kids, frozen in the parking area, mouths open, heads tilted, gathered close, telling them to wait there, fumbling for keys, racing to the door, hauling it open, leaping stairs, *Come on, come on*, stumbling on a few, scraping my knee and not feeling, *Shit, fuck*, hearing me sound like them, surprised, pushing myself to my feet and stretching my legs until they hurt, bounding faster, past the first landing and on to the next, grabbing the banister on one side, wall on the other, pulling, emerging in the center of shouts and screams, beside Jackie and Frank, who had backed away so far it would only take one step for them to leave, and I wanted them to, not explain, or apologize, just go. I caught a look at Wills. The cold feeling grew, his face was contorted, he looked monstrous, and it was everything I feared.

Ida's head poked from her front door, mouth gaping, head a small moon, thin hand clutching her dressing gown. I saw and ignored her, didn't want to know, that critical frown, her comprehending stare.

—What the hell's going on!

—Beverley, Jackie said.

I pushed by Frank, wanting to get between Wills and them. The big knife was in my son's hands and I felt a leap in my heart, wanted to cry out to him, but I couldn't.

—Mum, he said, and lowered the knife.

—Wills, what are you doing? What are you all doing? I said, not wanting to accuse, looking around.

—They're tryina chuck me out!

—We are not, Frank said. We're simply suggesting it might be better that he leaves!

—And what if I don't wanna! Wills screamed, raising the knife.

—Wills! Can you be quiet?

He glared at me, knife frozen, held high.

—Jackie, who are you to say who can and cannot stay in my house?

—We came around, she gulped, eyes sparkling. She'd been crying, was about to. Just to see if you both were all right, that's all. He was antagonistic from the very beginning . . .

—Big words, Wills said. *Fuck* your big words . . . Think I don't understand?

—And when we tried to have a discussion, he . . . he . . .

—He became aggressive, Frank said. He threatened my wife. Your sister. He said he'd slap her.

—She called me a liar!

—Okay, Wills? I think you should go inside.

—I'm not leavin you with them! So they can make up whatever story an twiss up your head!

—They won't twist up my head, Wills.

—How dare you suggest such a thing! Frank spluttered.

—They will! I can see it!

—Well I won't let them . . .

—I beg your pardon? Jackie said, and I saw I wasn't helping.

—Okay, how about we all go inside, stop broadcasting family business on the landing, and talk about this calmly, *without weapons*, I said, shooting Wills a stare. Surely we can do that?

—He's no family of ours, Jackie said. He's a feral child just like those kids you teach, and the sooner you see that the sooner you'll—

I don't know what happened. One minute I was between them and the next I'd been spun around, and he
was past me, and I heard Jackie scream, and the thud
of his body against Frank's, the second thud as Frank
hit the wall, and I was curled over the landing, dazed.
There was noise everywhere, but I recovered quick,
pushing myself up and leaping for him, throwing my
arms around his shoulders to pull him back, although of
course it'd been a bluff, he didn't want to stab her because if he did he'd had three or four seconds while I lay
against cold brick and Frank was slumped, three or four
when there was no one to stop him. And I saw it then,
just before I grabbed him, he'd stopped dead, stared at
Jackie, and when my arm went around his broad shoulders I accidently brushed his cheek, felt damp against
my forearms, and he was shaking, the knife level with
his hip.

I heard shouting from below, my kids. We had
swapped places. The shrill song came from down there,
silence above. Jackie stood, tall and erect, she reminded
me of our father. There was no fear, just sadness, and it
felt as though the big knife had been plunged into me,
only she did it with her eyes. I stood behind my son,
arms around his shoulders, breathing hard.

—I see, Jackie said. You'll get your wish, Beverley.
You won't see us again. Franklyn, come.

Frank got to his feet, eyeing us, drooping like a
clipped flower.

—Jackie, come on. There's no need—

—It's fine, Beverley. I understand.

She was down the stairs before I could say anything.
I didn't move, caught in the irony of getting what I asked

for and once again not wanting it somehow. The contradiction of wishing I could call my sister back, knowing I would not. That I missed her already, even while I wanted to protect my son and was angry with him, that I'd felt closer to Jackie in that one quiet moment than I had in years. I listened to the security door open and close, heard their voices, my kids. I was brought back to the moment, and I pulled him away.

Down the landing, Ida still watched. Damning me, I was sure. She heard the offbeat clatter of sneakers and shook her head, once. Closed the door.

—Go, I said to Wills, pushing him hard. Inside, now.

—I ain scared.

His eyes said different; said panic, doubt. The knife wavered.

—Go inside and put that away. Now!

There was an explosion of bodies at the peak of the stairs and I was looking right into their eyes: Grime, Chris, Jeff, and, of course, Sam. United. The girls behind, equally hard-eyed.

—Go home, guys, it's over.

—What's goin on, miss? Sam barked, and even though I was looking at him he wasn't seeing me, it was all Wills. His jaw was set, words mangled. His hand reaching behind him, all the boys poised that way.

—Sam. Go home.

—We can't, miss, not until we know you're cool, Grime said, and it was strange how calm he was in comparison with the others, mouths twisted like black-and-white gangsters. Grime looked relaxed, one hand on the rounded triangular bricks of the landing wall, the other pulling down his gray hood.

—I'm cool. Now go home. Thank you, but go home.

—Nah, miss, you don't look cool. Is this brudda troublin you? Chris said, and I saw the light meet his gold tooth. Even though I wasn't looking, I felt raised hackles. Turned and saw Wills, the knife, the glint. Pushed my palm toward him twice. *No.* Turned back.

—Guys, this is silly. There was an argument over nothing and it's done. You should go before you make it worse. I'm fine, I promise.

—Nah, miss, Jeff said. I don't think you heard right. Is this *nigga* botherin you?

My intake of breath, Jeff's mouth moving in that strange way, teeth and no lips, Wills's heat and my own instant anger, knowing he would say something stupid.

—Fuck you, man, your mum's a nigga, pussy'ole.

The group raised, moved forward as one. I stepped forward, arms wide.

—Hello! Hello!

Someone was shouting from the ground floor. Keeping between the kids and Wills, I inched to one side, peered over. A short man, blue shirt and dark vest, dark cap.

—The police are here.

—Community, Hayley said.

—You want to wait for the rest?

Sam squinted over my shoulder, backing up, bumping into the girls.

—Watch me, he said. Watch, brudda.

They turned and went, climbing to the landing above. They would wait it out. I leaned back over the wall, the officer was still calling.

—Hold on, I'll buzz you in. Hold on. I turned back to Wills. Go inside the house, now. I won't ask again.

He ducked his head, went without another word. I followed and picked up the intercom, hit the button.

❦

It was easy to see why my kids had such disdain for the community police. There were two, one white and disinterested, the other black and definitely interested, scanning my body with a wry smile, like the corner of his lip was caught on wire, pretending he was looking at his notes. They asked vague questions that either didn't deserve an answer or didn't need one, and it became clear they were there because they'd been called, not because they wanted to solve a crime. While we were talking about the nature of my dispute, me saying it was domestic, a family feud with my sister who had now left, my kids filed down in pairs, tossing sullen looks. The disinterested officer went over, searched the boys, found nothing, asked what they were doing, where they'd been. Of course they knew block residents, had perfect alibis. He let them go.

I listened to them walk across the parking lot, making noises like war cries. I answered the officers' questions, three of us trying to pretend we hadn't heard.

❦

They begin to move. After the hiatus of shock comes whispered swear words. Adrenaline leaves. Pain takes over. I see something, not far from me, and turn my head away, although of course I still hear it. There are moans, low at first, but they begin to grow in strength and I'm thankful because that means it isn't as bad as I thought, yet it doesn't stop the chill from snaking through my body, and I cover my mouth, try not to sob, listen against my will.

∞

Clear skies, clear streets. As above, so below. I'm not sure where the saying comes from, only that I read it, but the words seemed fitting in those moments, when the community police were walking across the parking lot and the night sky was painted red. I leaned over the landing wall. I needed a cigarette. The craving was a tingle on my lips, a tickle I couldn't really feel, but knew was there. I tried to calm myself. After all the noise, all my running, the hum of nothing was engaging, and I wanted to stay right there, where there were no people or sound, just my rapidly colliding thoughts. I leaned as far as I dared, felt cool brick against my belly and hung, not caring how I looked.

The flat, unlit, my head darting. Him on the sofa head down, hands between his legs, eyes closed, not moving, maybe praying. His lips opened and shut, so he must have been. I stood, not directly over him but to one side, and he knew I was there, I could tell, but he continued to chant, and I waited, found myself wishing I had my own mantra. My anger was building, clenched fingers and teeth, thinking the chants had come too late, and so I sat, and breathed again, and waited for him to finish. In a way I was grateful, because who knows what I may have said if he hadn't taken that time for himself.

Head raised. Open eyes. I sat on the edge of the easy

chair opposite, aware of the space. I forced the anguish down, forced neutrality.

—Are you all right?

A quick nod.

—I'm sorry you had to go through that. You know I wouldn't want it this way.

—Yeah, course, he said.

—At least we don't have to deal with the real police.

Nothing. I bit my lip.

—Can you tell me what happened?

I'd thought he might be reticent, but he looked up, as if he'd been waiting for me to arrive like Ida, and he turned his body, and told. He'd been watching a DVD when there was a knock at the door. When he answered, Jackie and Frank were there, asking for me. He told them where I was and, by his account, invited them in. They said yes. He'd thought something was wrong as soon as they entered; they were talking between themselves, roaming from room to room like they owned the place, making comments that hardly seemed appropriate—the potential of the flat as an economic boost, the growth of the area, the security precautions Stella McCartney's father had to make for her to move in down the road. Wills said nothing, offered tea. They declined, went to the living room and said they'd like to finish the conversation begun on their previous visit. Wills protested, told them it was better if I was there. Frank asked if he had anything to hide. Wills answered negatively, Jackie disagreed, and both parties seemed to get heated. Wills asked them to leave, go for a coffee and come back in half an hour. A reasonable request, he'd thought. They refused and said he was the one that should leave. He went to the door and opened it. They remained seated. In the exchange that followed Jackie called him a liar, and Wills did say that he'd slap her, he admitted, but it was an idle threat. That's all. Frank jumped up and tried to manhandle him, perhaps in an attempt to defend his wife's honor. Wills went into the kitchen, got the big knife, and emerged, pointed it at them. They got up pretty damn quick after that.

—But Wills, look, you were right up until then.

—Yeah.

His head fell, and I felt exasperated.

—I don't know why you kids do it. Your emotions rule, you can't live like that; once you've blown up you can't take it back. I'm all for passion, but come on . . .

—I've tried doing the cold thing. Detached. I can't.

—I'm not sayin you should be cold—

—Yeah you are. I can't be like that, like Jackie and Frank. Even them, they try an play like they don't care, but it's still there. You can force it back, you can't make it go away.

—Wills. I'm not saying you should be cold. Just that you can't let emotion rule your life. You're Buddhist. I thought you're meant to find Zen.

That stung, I could see. Fire burned.

—You talkin about me or your after-school youts? Them same youts that threatened me on your doorstep when I didn't do nuttin. I'm not them, you know.

—I know, but you're all my kids—

—I'm not. A *fuckin*. Kid.

And I saw him then; maybe for the first time. Sure, I'd taken note when he'd arrived, when he'd been sleeping, though that was colored by the warm tint of feeling, my joy at him finding me; my emotion, I allowed. Now I saw things I'd missed; his hands, large like bush leaves, the fleshy forearms and smooth width of his shoulders, like rolling green hills. The raw earth of his skin. The mistlike curl of his hair. He was wild as the land of our heritage, but that land was also lush, and gentle, welcoming and warm. There was all the harsh environment and soft nature of the continent in the boy who had knocked on my door, he couldn't help that. It flowed through him like black gold. Nothing would change that—his previous incarnation had already died, been crushed over time, liquefied until it became one with the physical form it sprung from.

I knew what I needed to do. What he wanted. I knew I should approach him. Place my hand on his neck and make him aware I was there. I should have, but the image of Ed stopped me, stiff legs and the lump climbing his pant leg. I wanted to tell Wills, couldn't think how to. How he would react. I was calm, maybe even Zen. Most of all, I was scared.

—Look, you're right. You're not a kid, and I've no right to treat you like one. Neither has my sister, certainly not Frank. We've had a pretty tough time, you more so than me, but both of us really. I think we should try not to involve other people, get to know each other. Me and you. What do you think?

—Yeah, he said, and this time I could see his tears.

—Okay. We'll do that. Get some sleep, okay?

—Cool. Thanks, Mum.

I got up and went into my bedroom. Shut the door, pulled the chest of drawers across it. I lay on the bed and couldn't sleep for worry.

❦

- I am safe.
- I am enough.
- I am strong.
- I am Me.

❦

It seemed Sue had found Zen. She scrutinized me, legs crossed. Frosted glass split gray sky into shards of light, piercing floorboards. Outside in her garden, birds sang.

—So why haven't you told him?

My shoulders twitched, limp.

—I don't know what to say. He might react badly, or emotionally, and I'm there in the house with him.

—Well, you may be able to force his hand. She thought, chin cupped in palm. What about Seth? He could be there.

—I can't ask. I've asked so much, and that could ruin it. With both of them.

—Beverley . . .

—I know what you're saying. Honestly. I know it seems like I'm handling this wrong, but you don't know these kids.

—I know you.

—That doesn't prove much.

—It proves you're stalling.

I smiled, nodding with her.

—Yes. Yes, I am. But supposing I get Seth to do it and Wills leaves; or he gets angry and Seth tries to throw

him out. What then? Seth has to go sometime. He knows
that. He could easily come back.

—I thought you said he wasn't like that.

—I *think*. I'm not sure. Of anything.

She lowered her head, rubbed her temple. I
gripped the armrest, rocked. Caught myself, Sue's
eyes. I wanted to tell her about my dream of fire, and
cane, and the spider mother, but that might have made
things worse.

—And Seth's not suspicious about the body?

—Not yet. He says that until they determine cause of
death, he fell. No case until then.

—I see . . . Foot tapping, leg wriggling. What about
the DNA test?

—What about it?

Sue gaped, professional air gone. I shifted in my seat.

—They sell them in Boots, apparently. It's a new
thing and they're quite cheap, thirty pounds.

She handed me a leaflet. Glossy, a woman and child.
I didn't look.

—Thanks. I'll think about it.

Sue's face closed. She almost gave me a dirty look.
Time for a new shrink, I decided.

❦

I went home, let myself in and picked up the cordless. I
didn't want to, but I had no choice. I had to try. It rang
once, clicked.

—Masters's residence, Patrick said.

My lip trembled. I held the cordless against my
breast, heard the squeak of his voice from the handset—

Hello, hello—knew I had to pull it together to stop my-self from flying apart, bursting into supernova a second time.

—Patrick.

He stopped then, and there was only the buzz and crackle of distance.

—Hello, Beverley. How are you?

—Not working?

—Yes. I work from home occasionally.

—You always preferred it.

—Yes.

—And how are things? Generally?

—Oh. Very good. They made me partner.

—I'm not surprised. Well done. You deserve it, you work so hard.

He shifted tone. Not entirely comfortable, less guarded, on safer ground.

—Thank you.

—I spoke with your son.

—Ah. Kumani.

Smiling despite himself, I could hear it.

—You didn't say.

—Yes. Well . . . we weren't sure what was appropriate.

—He's adorable. Belated congratulations. You both must be so pleased.

—Thank you.

—You're wondering why I'm calling.

—I was, actually, and I am in the middle of some-thing . . .

—You may have to put that aside.

He sniffed. Suspicion returned, enclosed in weighty silence.

—Now, Beverley, I know you feel you have something important to say, but you can't just—

—You must listen. I said it was urgent.

—And I called back.

—It doesn't matter, I said, sitting. Look, I may as well just say it. I've made contact with our son.

I waited. Even the crackles and buzzing were gone. I pushed the cordless against my ear, thought I caught something muffled; had he covered the mouthpiece? A thud, a scrape, and then it was there, like he was next to me. An uncontrolled whimper he tried to hold back, had been for years. He was crying. I'd made him cry.

—Why are you doing this?

—I'm not doing—

—Yes you are. You distress my wife, upset my son . . . Are you trying to disrupt my marriage?

—How dare—

—Seriously, do you want to break us up? Because I didn't do as you wished? I'm sorry about that, Beverley, but—

—You don't have to be sorry.

—It was wrong . . . At your father's funeral, for God's sake!

—Now hold on a minute. I think you need to get your facts straight. I didn't call to talk about our past; it was Rachelle who brought that up. I've come to terms with what we did. I happen to think it was one of our most beautiful moments. We let each other go, Patrick. That's what happened.

—Then why did you keep calling? I had to tell her in the end, she was already suspicious, and when you left those messages—

—I admit I was in a bad place. I've dealt with that, I really have. I'm much better. If you saw me, you'd know.

—Then why say that? About Malakay?

—Because it's true. Our son came home, and it's the most wonderful thing. He's handsome and intelligent and I just want you to know we're okay, I want you to come back and meet him and maybe we could all get to know each other, maybe even Rachelle and Kumani— we're all family, right? I think we should act that way, I mean who else do we have if not each other? Right?

I paused. Patrick was weeping. He was weeping openly and I hadn't heard. It came in waves, loud and soft, an expansive, desolate beach. He also had the continent inside him.

—Patrick?

—He's *dead*, Beverley! Some sick bastard took our son and he's dead! You're not well, Beverley, whatever you think. He was too young . . . too young . . .

He broke down. His sobbing was loud and hurt my ears. I held the phone out, looked at it. Put it back to my ear.

—Patrick?

The sobbing grew even louder.

—Patrick? I said. He is my son. And you'll be sorry.

I hung up. Stood, walked around the room. I went into the kitchen and poured a glass of water from the jug in the fridge, drank deeply. Set the glass in the sink, raised my eyes to the ceiling. Closed. Waited until the feeling passed and opened my eyes, went to the kitchen drawer. Took out the Post-its. Wrote a series in quick succession: *I am safe. I am enough. I am strong. I am Me.* I went around the house and put them in various positions.

Bathroom mirror. Bedroom wall. Beside the intercom. The last, *I am Me*, I placed in my journal, smoothing it down along the inside cover. I sat on the sofa and waited for him to come home.

⋙

The *pia mater*, often referred to as the *pia*, is the delicate innermost layer of the meninges. It is a thin, fibrous tissue, impermeable to liquid, which allows it to enclose cerebrospinal fluid. By containing this fluid the *pia mater* works with the other meningeal layers to protect and cushion the brain. The Latin means, literally, "tender mother."

⋙

I tried to hide it from him, should have known it was improbable. It permeated rooms, leaked from my pores, saturating the entire flat with blues funk, melancholy-stained blinds and curtains, the reek of discontent. I tried to be upbeat. I went shopping and made small talk with consumers, retail assistants, and even though we smiled and made nice, there was something veiled in their eyes, and if I dared to look over my shoulder as I left I'd see them whispering, or if they were alone they'd be watching. I would see their expressions in my mind's eye, a collection of static doubt, each reflecting my untethered mind state, each a response to me. I was tired, this is true, and I was also stressed. I developed pimples on my face, tender spots on my back and neck. My body wouldn't move the way I wanted. I bumped into things, regularly. I lost things, almost on a daily basis. I forgot things, put food in the oven and remembered I'd done so too late, put clothes in the washing machine and only thought about it days after, took my journal out to write and moments later couldn't find it, had to search the whole flat. I would have gone to Sue, usually, but I wanted to get through on my own. If I wasn't well, as Patrick had said, there would be no bailout. I would face the prospect head-on, make it better.

I tried to hide it, yet he noticed; probably as soon as he came back that night. The change had fallen between us like a wriggling fish spat from clear sky, dancing and mouthing at us. We turned from it, from each other. Wills inside his room, I in mine. We ate together, sometimes even watched TV together, but we never spoke of the lone fish on the living room floor, even though it flapped enough to flick water in our eye. Seth called, repeatedly. I sent texts to reassure him, never called back. I had hurt too many people.

One day I emerged from my room and he was there, sitting with a book in his hands; one of mine, *When Gods Lived*. He seemed intent and I didn't want to disturb him. He laid the book flat on his knees.

—Mornin.

—Morning, Wills. I thought you'd be at Vicky's.

—Not on the weekend.

—Oh. Don't you usually go out anyway?

—Yeah.

He closed the book, turned it in his hands.

—Well, you don't have to.

—I jus thought maybe I should stay. Do that gettin-to-know-you thing?

—Right.

I sat next to him. We grinned like shy teenagers.

—Weird, innit?

—Very. I think I've been avoiding it.

He winced.

—You mean me?

—Of course not.

—Yeah it is. Ever since that night.

I took his big hand, covered it with both of mine.

—That's not true. I just want to give you space. It's not the biggest flat, and we could easily get on top of one another. If you're going to stay, I can't be in your face. That's my thinking anyway.

He looked around the flat as though blinded by direct sunlight.

—What's with the Post-its?

—What do you mean?

—You changed them.

Damn. So wrapped up in me I hadn't thought that they'd be read. So used to being alone.

—Yes. Well, I think I need positive reinforcement. I've been feeling bad, it's actually nothing to do with you, more with time, my relationship with my sister, that sort of thing. So they're the same type of message, just more personal. I hope you don't mind.

—Oh nah, not at all, he said.

We sat, my two hands wrapped around his one. It felt nice. We'd never touched before.

—I can take them down if it does.

—Nah. I was jus thinkin, he said, and then he did. For a long while. He started, came back. I was thinkin it might be good. To write things down.

—It would, I said. I have notebooks. I could give you one.

—Safe.

—That's okay.

My hand was growing sweaty. I didn't want to take it away, lose the feeling.

—I didn't say nuttin before but I wanned to. Thanks. For believing me.

I cried then. Couldn't help it, or stop, the tears just came. I shook, holding Wills's hand, trying to contain the energy, but it only grew. At first, he simply watched me, his face like a judge. Then he reached out, touched my head. Afro-comb fingers, thin, poking into my scalp, raking hair. It was hardly comforting but it was the first time he'd touched me of his own accord and I felt relieved, also terrible, because of what I hadn't told.

—It's okay, Wills said. It'll be all right.

I barked a laugh at the absurdity of our reversal, and he gave a small boy smile, thinking he'd done well.

—It must have been hard, he said. All them years.

—Yes, I whispered. My voice was hoarse.

—No one believes you.

—Yes, I cried, stilted warmth against my cheeks.

—Thanks for sticking by me.

I wept harder, turned, threw my arms around him. He held me and we cried together, me loud, him virtually silent. We felt good, we felt strong, we felt us. His arms were awkward, not nearly close enough, and I didn't mind. The sounds and voices of the outside world fell back into a mute echo.

I let go. He was solid, facing the opposite wall, eyes damp, not making a sound. His cheeks gleamed.

He trembled. I sat up, clearing my throat. Arranged my clothes, made space between us.

—I have something to tell you.

Red-tinged eyes. Nearly enough to stop me.

—I took the keys. I went to Parson's Green. To Eddie's.

His eyes darted, found resolve, returned.

—So you spoke? You didn't say.

—I know I didn't. I'm sorry. I went on the spur of the moment, it wasn't planned.

He was looking at me strangely, and I was reminded of the whispers, faces I'd seen that knew me. It made me nervous.

—You spoke then? What did he say?

I took a deep breath, clasped his hand again.

—I went up and knocked on the door but he didn't answer. I let myself in and found him. He'd passed away, Wills. I'm sorry.

The red-tinged eyes were probing, searching me, and it was like nothing I had known, they made my skin crawl. It was subtraction, one into none. It was life-less. He pulled his hand from mine, slowly, verging on tenderness; let it rest in his lap. He stared into space. I didn't know what to say, where to look.

—I'm so sorry.

—Is he still there?

—No. Sharp regret, low in my body. I called the police.

Head bowed. My feet turned inward. I hadn't noticed before. Wills felt rigid beside me.

—So how will I know what happened?

—They'll tell me. I know someone . . . He dealt with my case, from before . . . He knows.

Shaking his head, lips twisted.

—You lied.

—Not to hurt you! I just . . . I didn't know what to say.

—All right, he said. All right.

Lost in thought, hands in his lap, he sat on the sofa edge.

—So what do you want to do?

—I better go. Find out what happened.

—But you can't—

—I have to.

—It won't solve anything.

—I have to see.

He stood up.

—Don't. It's not good for you.

—Beverley. I have to.

I clamped down on my lip to stop the welling inside me. *Beverley.* I reached for his hand but he pulled away.

—Wills, let's wait. I'll call my friend and we'll have him come around and we can find out what happened. You can ask anything.

—I gotta go, Wills said, and he was rushing around me, spinning me. He marched toward what he'd spied, my open bag, and dug out the contents, dragging them onto the dining table. I leaped over.

—Hey! What are you doing? You can't go through my things!

—You go through mine, he said.

I heard my own voice and put a hand to my throat as if to make contact with the place such nonsense had emerged from.

—All right. Let's slow down a little . . .

—I gotta go, Wills said.

He walked to a cupboard, opened the door, and found my coats. His arm snaked in, stayed prone, snaked out, and he had them, the keys, jangling in his palm. He turned toward me.

—I ain vex. I jus gotta find out.

He paced by me while I absorbed the words, and I lost my nerve and panicked, and it was as though all the years since had no meaning, and in the time it took to make those steps I was the monster, and there was nothing else but his broad back. I heard a terrible noise, but it was only when it was done that I realized I was the owner. I ran, and reached out, hauled him back. There was a quick view of something dark, a flicker of feeling against my eyelid and a hard thump against the side of my face, and I was reeling, bright flashes before me even though my eyes were shut. I ducked, held my hands over my face.

—*Fuck!* I heard, from somewhere above.

I stumbled, fell. Hands around my shoulders and he was there, next to me, helping me to my feet. He led me in an unknown direction and the pain was still enough to make me gasp, spasms of color before my eyes. He took my hand, guided my fingers and I felt them touch something soft, even while I noted how much his had changed, not stiff and comblike, but warm and yielding, and he turned me gently so I could sit, which I did one-handed.

The pain hadn't subsided; its treble was being countered by a deep bass, a throb that was temperate and raw, would intensify. I could feel its bloated promise even then. My body dipped toward his weight as he joined me.

—I'm sorry. I didn't mean it.

—I know, I croaked. I know.

—I just lashed out. I didn't mean it.

—It's okay, I smiled. Silly us. You might need to get some ice.

He left in a rush. I was shaking. A tiny voice in my head said I should be grateful for the blow, for what it had chased away. If he hadn't struck me, worse might have happened. The monster might have been raging about the flat. I breathed myself back in little portions. When he returned with the bag of ice wrapped in a towel, I patted the seat beside me.

—Sit.

He did. I reached for the towel.

—Nah. Let me.

I removed my hand. The light hurt my eye, and I gasped. He pressed the towel against my face. I gasped louder.

—*Shit . . .*

—Hold still, he said. D'you wanna grab it?

—Yes.

—Okay, go on.

I placed a hand on his. He started to pull away and I pushed hard, yelped again. He kept his hand on the towel. The ice felt good, added a pleasant sting to the pain.

—Sorry.

—Stop saying that. It was my fault.

—Yeah, well, I shouldn't have lashed out.

—And I shouldn't have grabbed you. Even stevens.

We were silent, my fingers growing numb.

—Wills?

—Yeah.

—No matter what happens, I love you. More than anything. I love you.

—Yeah, I know, he said. I love you too.

—Good, I said. And I couldn't stop smiling.

✑

Our thoughts are not the substance of reality, but its shadow.
—Jean-Luc Goddard

✑

Kaleidoscopic colors churned, merging when I closed my right eye, bursting when I opened it. Sunlight hurt, so I covered the eye with cotton wool and a rectangular pad, stepped onto the landing with a rigid hand on my brow, saluting the world. Of course, the first person we saw was Ida. We stood dead still, waiting for her to lift her broom, go inside. The door slammed. I squeezed Wills's arm and prayed for courage.

At the hospital, my son on my arm like a suitor, I was given a large rectangle patch, a prescription for white fluffy cream. Halfway home I stopped at the organic shop for a tub of arnica, and when we reached the flat I put the fluffy cream in a cupboard, still bagged. The bass throb was excruciating and I sometimes opened my mouth to expel pain, caught myself as Wills noticed and blew out slow, like releasing air from a shaken bottle of soda. His remorse was obvious. In the market he had bought vegetables, meat, packets of sauce; with my money, admittedly, but he seemed clear about what he wanted.

That evening, when he couldn't stand to listen any longer, he went into the kitchen and chopped and sautéed until a glorious smell arose. Within half an hour he came into the living room with a plate on a tray, juice in a cup. I sat back, took the food. A Thai red curry, beef and pak choi. I tried not to seem surprised, but he saw my expression and laughed. I ate, amazed. It was as good as any restaurant.

—Where did you learn *this*?

—Vicky.

—Figures, I said, and he rolled his eyes, grinned, went for his own tray.

It was like that for two whole days. I didn't ask if Wills was going to the Parson's Green flat, and he didn't leave. He made breakfast, lunch, and dinner, changed my dressing, even produced DVDs from somewhere, simple Hollywood blockbusters, but they passed time. We played board games, *Scrabble* and *Monopoly*. He wasn't very good, although we had fun. We talked, not about the past, our traumas and mistrust, but about ourselves, what we liked to do, people we had known and loved; and somewhat unconsciously, we spoke of family. I brought out photo albums, old ones, made before it all happened, filled with pictures of my mother and father, my aunts and uncles and cousins back home. We flicked through stiff pages and I spoke about his aunt as a child, his grandfather as a young man; I even admitted to my difficult relationship with his grandmother, something I hadn't told anyone, not even Ida. It was the most perfect forty-eight hours. I smiled a great deal, though it caused pain, and I relished those moments, knowing they would end.

When the third night came, just around twilight, I got up from the sofa that had become my camp. He watched, and I could feel his thoughts. I went into the bathroom and stood before the mirror, detached the rectangular pad, lifted and examined. I sighed. The arnica had done some good, brought the swelling down, but my skin shone red and was tight across my cheek, and it was a bruise, there was no mistaking that. My right eye was half closed, yellow with injury. I replaced the pad, regarding myself.

I wasn't sure what would be worse, to stay or go. I went into the living room, stood before him.

—Is it bad?

I lowered my head, nodded. He puffed, cheeks round as a jazz trombonist's. Emptied.

—What you gonna do?

—I think I should go. It might be better.

He put his cap on, lay back.

—Yeah.

—I'll talk to them.

—Yeah.

—Let them know it was an accident. If I don't go, they'll make up their own story, and we don't want that.

—No.

I wanted to hug him, didn't. It would become a self-fulfilling prophesy if I let it, I remember telling myself, better to act like it was a normal night, me raring to go, to see my kids and find out how their week had been.

—I'll just get ready then.

—No problem.

I changed into casual clothes and went back. He was still there, cap low, still thinking.

—Do you want me to leave?

—Definitely not. You stay put, do you hear me? Too strident. He said nothing, just looked. I'm sorry.

—It's cool. I won't leave you, Mum.

I tried not to choke, stood as still as I dared for many moments, pulling everything in, toward myself, so nothing would leak when I left for the outside world, when I walked, when I reached the club. I waited, didn't care how long it took, or that Wills was studying me like a hieroglyphic, eyebrows low, trying to decipher my meaning. I waited. And when it was all close, tight, and cloying around me, when I felt there was no more than the exterior shell, everything enclosed, I stood straight and smiled again, and breathed out.

—Okay, I said. I'm going. Lock the door.

—Cool.

—See you later, I said.

The landing seemed desolate, still. No neighbors, no Ida. No leaflets poking through letter boxes, or bin liners beside doormats. No empty Abel & Cole boxes. The streets were quiet too, soft rain, no kids on the corner, people walking hunched, hoods hiding faces, umbrellas hiding faces. The quiet hush of passing cars. Shadows and bulked forms. Dull smudges of street and shop lights as if flattened by a thumb; whites, oranges, yellows. The clouds reflected worldly light and there was no wind, it was actually warm, and the rain cooled my face, felt good against my skin, my rectangular pad.

No one outside the club. Inside, the rapid vibration

of taut energy, the echo of raised voices brought to an abrupt halt, bodies stalled in midmotion, several changes of direction, toward the door, toward me, the hush as I entered. And I had known what they would do, had known what was coming, just as I knew exactly what was in the air when I stepped onto the landing: a night of wind and rain, of thick, everlasting cloud, the constant tap of the world against glass. The trickle of water, earthbound.

I kept walking toward the desk, ignoring the silence, put my folder down, wiped at the green board even though I never used it, faced them. They had seen through my shabby theatrics. I cursed myself for making it obvious, letting them know the change had come.

—Evening, everybody.

No reply. No eye contact. No sound.

—Is nobody going to speak! I said, smile bright, and amazingly enough, I actually *did* feel good. For the first time in a long while I was happy to be in class, happy to be going home after, if I could have only closed my eyes and not seen them.

—Depends what you wanna talk about, Chris said. I was surprised to see him sneer, the way he eyed me. My shoulders collapsed. I sat on the table.

—Okay. Okay, I suppose we should discuss the previous night . . .

Sam wasn't there, I realized, as I risked a look. He wasn't there but everyone else was, and that frightened me. Grime sat on a table, pose matching mine, watching. Again he looked calm, eyes half closed, maybe he'd been smoking.

—What's to discuss? Heshima said, and laughed.

—Well, obviously odd things were occurring at my place . . .

—Sure bloody, someone said, I couldn't tell who, and the class erupted into spewed chatter.

—Guys? Guys?

They wouldn't stop. A burst of voices combined to form pressure. It hurt my ears. Grime stood.

—Hold up, man, hold up. One at a time, yeah? One at a time. How we gonna know wha gwaan if we don't let her speak?

The kids fell silent. I willed my fingers not to touch the pad, and they ached to rebel. Grime was still standing.

—What I wanna know, miss, is what's up with the dude you got in your yard? Wha gwaan wiv that?

More noise. I closed my eyes, covered my ears.

—Let her speak! Let her speak! Jeff bellowed.

I waited for them to quiet, pushed off from the table.

—Okay. I know you guys are owed an explanation. That's only fair. And I know there are vicious rumors going around, which I am under some obligation to refute. But this is my life here, my private life—

Eruption. Noise. I raised my voice.

—And I'm going to let you know right here and now that I only go so far. Do you hear me? I'll only say as much as I feel is right for you to know, because after all, you're my kids . . .

They began to bang tables. I looked toward the door.

—Class! Will you stop that this minute! Stop at once!

Tendons protruding, face hot. My body craned forward, nearly on tiptoes. They were silent. Closed faces. I heard something, saw another tutor by the open door, the woman who taught computing, who I never spoke to. She was at the threshold, ready to bark, until she saw me.

—Everything okay?

—Yes, I said. Fine.

—Sure?

—Positive. Really.

She nodded once, disappeared like a genie. I eased myself back onto the desk.

—Now come on, guys. This is me you're talking to. You're my kids. And I know you might have good reason to feel otherwise after last week, but that was a bad moment, my first in however long, and you can't hold it against me. It's a family issue . . .

—So how's man family? Jeff spat.

—That's not what I meant.

—Ain we your family?

—Miss, you're confusing us, Vanessa said, and I felt terrible.

—You're not supposed to have man outside your house wiv a *shank*, Chris said, the others slapping his palm, one after the other, brisk contact echoing throughout the room. We're not supposed to come an see how you are an find man beddin down in your flat like he come stay a few.

—Supposed to be showin us how to stay *off* road an miss is more road than us! Hayley said, to more laughter. I felt myself glare at her until she noticed, and was shocked.

—Miss is slipping, I heard from someone, again I couldn't tell who.

—Now listen, I know it might seem odd—

—Seriously, miss, who *is* that brer, cos I tell you sut-tin right now, I don't *like* him . . .

Jeff, eyeing me with the look in his eyes I hated, until Grime banged the table.

—Let her speak! Let her speak!

Silence. I wanted to cry, gulped hard.

—All right. I know how it might seem. And I apolo-gize on Wills's behalf for what happened between you all. He was heated, everyone was heated, and if it wasn't for my sister you never would have seen all of that. And I'm sorry. That's my family issue, and truly, it should never have happened. But it did, and so we have to deal with it, okay? About Wills, all I can say right now is he's someone I've known for a long time, and he's staying at my flat until his circumstances become better. That's it. Maybe I'll tell you more over time, but that's it because it's my business. And I know how you all feel. I truly ap-preciate it. You don't know how good it is to know you're all willing to run up those stairs to my rescue like that. It feels great. But I don't need saving, that's the trouble, and I love you all but you're making a big mistake . . .

One voice, then two, and then they were all speaking at once, all shouting, and I was overwhelmed.

—Miss, *you're* makin the mistake, man . . .

—This a joke. Truss, this is a joke, man, I can see wha gwaan!

—Look at her face! Look at her face an tell me suttin!

—Fam need to know, you better show man! Show man an watch!

—Miss, this ain right, you better see about this dude, you ain thinkin straight—

Jeff banged his palm on the desk, jumped up.

—Hear what! Hear what! he shouted, until there was silence again. What I wanna know is, wha gwaan wiv that eye, cos I know say that's what everyone wants to hear bout!

Uproar. I stood, screamed.

—Stop it! Stop it, all of you! Now, I don't know what you've been told, and who you've been told by, although I suspect I know, but this has nothing to do with him—

—Tell the truth, miss, Jeff said. Tell the truth, you're pipin that yout, innit?

The girls, Hayley and Heshima, laughing, covering their mouths, faces red, trembling with mirth. Vanessa, watching me, mouth a hard thin line, shaking her head.

—What do you mean? Piping? I don't . . . Getting it, words sinking in. How dare you?

—Don't go on like you don't like a bit, Heshima said, disdain flooding her face. Hench nigga like that.

—Don't you *dare* use that word in my class!

—You can't tell me nuttin, she said, and snapped and chewed her gum. Not after you're bangin some yout.

Chris also stood, side by side with Jeff and Grime.

—Seriously, miss, you gonna let man do you like that? Buss up your eye?

—This was an accident! I left a cupboard door open and I turned and got hit in the eye! I did it myself!

The whole class laughing, falling about tables, stomping feet, clapping hands, and giving each other dazed looks of amazement, all except Chris and Grime. They stood fully upright, staring, and I had to look away. I had failed. I had performed a foul I couldn't take back. Their arms folded, they spoke in whispers. They began to leave.

—Chris, Lucien! Where are you going?

—Class done, miss, done know. Goin home.

Grime swung around, eyeballed me, and I knew. He walked out. The others were swinging backpacks onto shoulders, packing away books, pulling baseball caps over their eyes.

—Hey, guys. Come on, guys, don't be this way. We can talk.

—Nuttin to talk about, miss, Hayley said. Them lot done made up their mind, innit?

—What do you mean by that? I don't get you.

—That's the trouble, miss, innit? Heshima said. You don't get us. That's what we're trying to say.

They left, all of them, more or less in single file, Hayley, Heshima, and Jeff, Vanessa last. She turned, just before she walked out the door, and whether it was sorrow or pity in her eyes I couldn't tell. I remembered I'd never once walked her home and the suddenness of the thought shook me, and then she was gone, leaving me with a desperate desire to chase them, to try and say more, convince them. The resulting silence, once the room had emptied, was louder than their shouts. I slipped from the desk, pulled out the chair, sat. I cradled my head in my hands, mindful of the pad, hoping one of my kids might return, but she never did.

❧

The sounds scare me. In my own home, they scare me. I don't want to hear whimpers, the groans. Don't want to hear the shuffle outside my door, or squawking gossip-hungry vultures, eager for bones to pick. Most of all I don't want to see, and so I shroud myself in darkness, reach out and draw it close, covering me.

❧

I slammed the front door, dripped rain onto floorboards, trotting into the flat. Not in the living room. Not the kitchen. I walked to his closed bedroom door. I pressed my ear against wood. I knocked.

—Hello . . .

Wills lay on the single bed, one leg propped on the other, still reading. He sat up when he saw me.

—What happened?

—The kids, they're angry. Because of what happened. And this, when I came into class with this, they went crazy.

He got up, slow, not coming near me.

—What did you tell them?

—Nothing, just that you're a friend staying with me.

—Not why? Who I am?

—Well— I stopped, looked at the ceiling. I don't think it's their business. Everyone knows everything around here and I don't like the idea of my affairs being discussed in every coffee shop in town. I'd rather have a private life.

—Well, no wonder, Wills said. If I was in your class I'd be vex too.

I shut my mouth, touched the pad.

—Ow, I said. We laughed.

—Look, all I'm sayin is they don't know nothin, jus I'm some guy who attacked your sister on the landin, an punched you in the face. I'm sayin, if it was me I'd be thinkin I'd wanna word with that kinda guy, see what he's about.

—That's very understanding, but it doesn't mean—

—I'm gonna talk to them. Explain. I don't reckon they want beef. They're your kids, innit?

Those eyes, so wide, so sincere. He was trying. With all his might he was trying.

—Yes, but you must be aware they have troubled home lives, I said, stumbling on my words.

—I understand, Wills said.

—Yes. Yes, of course you do.

—Don't worry about it. We'll wait, an when they come I'll explain the whole thing. If it's got this bad they need to know.

He looked so sure, tall and calm, a rock.

—I was actually thinking you were right; maybe you should leave.

He stared at me.

—Not for good. And not if you really don't want to. I'm not trying to throw you out, please believe me. I love you. I just don't want you to come to harm.

Wills relaxed, slipped hands into pockets.

—I'm not goin nowhere.

—But maybe it would be better? To go to Vicky's?

—I can't.

—Or one of your other places? Or I could give you some money for a B&B, just for a few nights? For me?

Wills shook his head.

—Nah, it's all right. You think I'm gonna fly out knowin mans comin to my mum's on alms? Not at all. I'm staying right here.

I wilted then, and moved away a few steps.

—All right then, I said. Whatever you say.

I went to the front door, turned all the locks. Made sure the windows were shut tight and the phone worked. I checked the flat for weapons; all I had was the wrench and the big knife. I hid them beneath the sofa cushion, where Wills wouldn't find them, but I could. Seth was on my mind, had called again and again. I had been dodging him, but sent a lengthy text, explained everything was fine; I just needed peace and quiet, time alone with my son.

Wills came out for the first hour. When nothing happened he went into the kitchen to heat some chicken he'd baked. He came back out with four golden thighs on a small plate, offered it. I took the plate. He went back into his bedroom, book in hand, keeping the page with his thumb and forefinger. I stared at the plate. I wasn't hungry, knew I should eat. I kept seeing Heshima laughing, face flushed, Vanessa shaking her head and looking at me. It made me want to gag, but I picked up the chicken and made myself bite, forgot myself when the taste hit, began to respond to that rather than my first, mechanical urge, to eat because it was there. I finished the thighs too quickly, wiped my greasy mouth, lay back.

Rain fell in earnest, like the clouds meant it. The patter of water hit the roof and rolled from the landing, creating a continuous applause directly outside my window. How nice to be indoors, in warmth. How nice to have my son, to be able to shield him from the wet and cold not five paces from where I sat. It was a mother's right, a mother's gift. To protect him from the elements, keep him safe. And if she couldn't perform that simple task, what use was she? None, I told myself, grabbing the nearest blanket and wrapping it around me. None at all.

It was a bond formed in the first minute. In my colostrum, breastfed at birth, my body attempting to protect him, boost his immune system against pathogens. What troubled me was not natural inclination, made apparent long before my son was abducted; rather, the length of time I had not been a mother, in the truest sense of the word.

Without Malakay my breasts leaked without pause. I wore cotton pads, much like the one that covered my eye, to catch thick liquid. They ached from fullness, and often kept me up at night, when Malakay had fed most. Then, after weeks of draining myself to get to sleep, I stopped producing milk. Although the doctors warned it might happen, although I had willed the stretched tightness to go away, I was distraught, devastated. My milk had dried up because my son wasn't there. Of course, I never showed any pain. I retreated to the bedroom, let the doctor squeeze my breasts, kept it in my gut. I had seen my mother's worry, I can admit I wanted more. She had offered advice to keep me healthy for Malakay's return: foods to eat, supplements to drink, rest I had to take. Yet when the colostrum stopped flowing, my mother patted my hand and told me it was a good thing. I never forgave her for that.

I'd been twelve when I first began to grow. Nubs on my chest, sore to the touch, tender as the flesh beneath nails. I guessed what they were from constant study, and Jackie, whose nubs had blossomed into a pair that rivaled most grown women, round and firm, bursting from her clothes no matter what she wore. Mine were different. When they reached maturity they were small, pointing outward with a confidence that outweighed their actual size; unclothed, they dropped slightly, unsure. At twelve, I was full of their unknown potential, ready to join the ranks of womanhood with contenders to rival anyone. I was ecstatic, looked at them all the time, touched them, rubbed them against things, walls, fences, sometimes even boys, discussed them with classmates, lifted clothes and compared. Yet my mother said nothing.

I tried to talk with Jackie, but she was too busy in her own world with her own friends and so she brushed me aside. I would have asked my father, but my growing breasts was our first encounter with new territory, with the realm that had clearly mounted boundaries stating no entry, leaving my father on the outskirts, sad-eyed. I gritted my teeth, entered the hostile country alone. And my mother said nothing.

I came into the kitchen one summer to find Mum with Jackie. They were laughing, open boxes on the dining table, pink and purple crepe paper falling softly to the floor, holding bras against their chests, sashaying like models. The bras were beautiful, lace and flowers, pastel colors, huge. When I walked in they stopped laughing, put the bras back in their boxes, and closed lids. Mum asked what I'd like for lunch. I tried to get them to talk about what I'd seen, but they refused. Months later, when I became too big to ignore, my father took me to Debenhams for my first fitting.

Later, I would wonder whether my mother's negligence was passed down, inherited like her long legs, her cane complexion. I would wonder whether I was a mother at all.

When I saw my sister, I saw her. They even had the same gray eyes. I'd always known that, but I'd never been conscious of it. The thought was clarified somewhere else, somewhere within me, and then Wills's face floated in my mind like a specter, and I realized how much like my father he was, especially when he smiled. I saw my dream, the side-winding flash of leaping flames, the bark of dogs, my sister, father, and mother, and I was there, in the shadow of cane, spread-eagled in her web, darkness that might have verged on complete if it wasn't for the gleam of the quartz moon. Leaves sighed in reluctant unison, expelling life force so I could breathe in, breath out, so they could do the same. The voice of the cane was a hum on the edge of my hearing. I hung and relaxed and then I heard something else, when I was comfortable with the gentle swaying that hardly moved me, yet I felt it, as the cane sentinels on either side bent with the breeze, and when I became still, there it was: the crash, the crescendo, the sound of death on glistening rocks and pebbles, the drawing back, the gathering; the sea. I smiled as I swung in the dark that enveloped me, I embraced blackness within and without and I let go, content just to hang, and be. I heard my salvation, my calling, and recognized the words. It was the gospel according to cane.

The banging was like the crash of surf against rocks; I liked it, turned over, blanket pulled tight around my shoulders until I realized it wasn't inside my head, it was out in the world, and my eyes opened, and I became aware of pressure on my shoulder, and when I looked, Wills was there, eyes bright.

—They're here, he said.

I threw the blanket aside. The door was shaking, fit-ful, gathered forms made opaque in the dimpled glass window. There were voices, bangs. I was awake.

—What are you doing! I shouted.

—Let us in or we kick it off!

Jeff. I wanted to kill him.

—How dare you come barging into my house!

—Let us in!

Another deep rattle. Wills grabbed my arm.

—Do it, he said. Let them in.

—Stay back, I told him, and switched off all the lights so there was nothing but the glow from the landing.

I went to the door, unlocked. Before I could turn the latch fully, they pushed at the door, tried to rush past. I kept ahead of them, backing off. Jeff, Grime, Chris, Sam. I could tell from their voices and heights, strangely enough even from their smell, though I couldn't see. I backed down the passage, past the intercom, into the living room. Sam peeled back his hood. His eyes were black holes, vacant in half-light. He stared at Wills.

—All right, brudda, you gotta come out.

—Sam? Who the hell do you think you are, coming in here like this? This is my *home*.

—That's why he's gotta leave, Chris said. If he goes, we'll go. If he don't . . .

—If he doesn't, what? What?!

—You know what, Jeff said.

Grime said nothing. He stared at Wills and smiled. I kept my eyes on him.

—I don't believe you. Any of you. I try to teach you right, week in and out, open my home . . .

—Yeah, well, you shouldn't open your yard to everyone, miss, Sam said, and he was in tears. They rolled
down his face and fell from his chin, but he wouldn't
wipe them. Look at your face! Look at what he done, an
you're tryin to protect this *fucker* . . .

—All right, all right, Wills said.

I saw them tense. The fire that had been tamed by
Sam's tears came back into his eyes. I poised, ready to
leap.

—Shut the fuck up, bruv!

—Let him speak, don't you even want to hear what
he's got to say? How brave!

—Jeff, Sam said. Back off, yeah? Jeff narrowed his
eyes at him, didn't respond. Wha you gotta say, bredrin?
One chance, that's it.

He waited. We all waited. Wills raised his hands.

—Look, I know how you man feel. I get it. I'd be
heated too, in your shoes. But you don't know what's
goin on, really. An I apologize if I offended you, yeah? I
was outta order. Vex. An the reason I was vex is cos they
tried to dash me out the yard when I'm her son, bredrin.
I'm her son come back to live with her, so I can't go.

Heads lowered, hands dropped by their sides. Grime
was turned to the window, so I watched Sam. His chest
was rising and falling, faster and faster, and when he
raised his head he scared me so much I gasped, audibly.

—That makes it *worse*, he said, and then it was in his
hand, a thick, curved knife, and his face grimaced, and
he stepped toward us.

I howled and moved, crouched, picked up the first
thing I could find, my small coffee table, threw it. My
fingers bent, pain arced through my left hand. I heard

a thud and clatter as it hit someone, muffled swearing, and then there were all bodies, and gasps and thumps like someone beating dust from cushions in a backyard, and struggle, and cries of pain, the crack of fists against bone. I couldn't see Wills or hear him. I was pushed away, intentionally it felt like, spun across the room, and I crashed into my big coffee table, the one in front of the sofa, sending tea mats and magazines everywhere, hearing it break. I got up immediately. Orange light on writhing movement, no heads or limbs, one seething mass, *I got im, I got im!* A terrible sound, a low *snick* that reminded me of dismembering chicken, a howl, long and unrestrained, and I was up again, I was searching under the sofa cushion, I was finding the big knife and I was bounding over furniture, reaching the mass, feeling for the thick material of outdoor coats, and whenever I found it, letting the knife plunge, hearing cries, pulling them off with all my strength, away from him until there was only one, and I held him by the collar, turned him and put it in him, felt momentary resistance and give, and it slid inside easily, and I felt warmth on my wrist from the others, and hot breath on my face, and I pulled it out just as smooth and he collapsed onto my floorboards, and it was only then that I had time to think I might have been wrong, I might have stabbed the wrong boy, and I threw the knife aside, disgusted, scrabbled around on my floor, and the groans began around me.

—Wills, I cried. Wills!

—I'm here, I heard beneath me. Something was wrong, his voice was garbled, and when I put a hand down I felt more blood, and he roared.

—Oh, my boy, I said, and cradled his face, and it was sticky. Oh, my boy, I'm so sorry. So sorry.

He tried to speak, couldn't. I jumped up, ran for the cordless, and dialed Seth. I left the lights off until they came.

❧

Voices outside my door, sharp to whispered, but no one knocks, just the authoritarian rattle of the letter box, and I know it's him. I open and let Seth walk inside, shivering slightly. Adrenaline, Sue would say. My clothes feel clammy and the warmth of the blood is cold now, but I don't want to change, to leave. The moans have faded into silence, only our voices.

—Can we have some light?

—No, I say quickly. Please.

—Okay. Okay.

He comes further inside, looks around. In the dull light I can see him crouch beside their prone bodies, can hear quick cries and the pant of breath.

—Did you check them yet?

—No.

—Okay. No worries, he says. I can tell that's a lie.

—What are we going to do?

—The ambulance is on its way, he says, standing. I've got some people coming, friends. They'll need to talk with you.

My mouth works, shock robs my voice.

—But . . . I thought we'd sort it out . . .

—I had to call it in, Bev.

—I thought *you'd* sort it out.

—It's too much, Seth says. I had to call it in. Sorry.

I sit by Wills. He's breathing in quick gasps, and the towel I wrapped around his leg is sodden. I stroke his sweaty head.

—If it's any consolation, this looks like a clear No Further Action. It'll be all right.

I nod, look into my son's face.

—Yes, I say. It will.

Blue light, bouncing from wall to wall. Seth crouches next to me, pulls me toward him. We hug.

❦

If you don't hear, you must feel.
—West Indian Mother's Proverb

❦

And I thought I knew silence. Maybe I had. It might have been that what I'd heard was as quiet as my surroundings got, and so I became accustomed to ongoing noise: the slam of a car door, a distant shout, faraway music, fading into nothing—the lonely cry of sirens. Sometimes, in the city, I had woken during the night, marveled at nothingness, but even then there was something expectant, something pending, waiting for lights, kettles to warm, radios. Family chatter.

Here, there is nothing. The darkness is unbroken. The silence is full, unchecked, and some nights I lie in bed and feel as though I am falling a million miles in no sure direction. I smile in darkness, I smile and feel it. Human beings have always envied birds their flight.

In daylight, there are rolling fields, darting rabbits, sheep that run whenever we come close. After a fence, at the very bottom of the hill, cows munch grass and drink from a small pond. There is a Doberman, Tamar, who I happen to believe secretly loves us. He belongs to the owners, Kate and Malcolm. There is a greenhouse full of tulips, tables and chairs on the front lawn. I spend many mornings outside, eating my breakfast and writing.

That's what I'm doing when I hear the swing of the electric gate and the bonfire crackle of gravel; see a car roll down the driveway. It parks alongside mine. When the door opens and Seth gets out, I put down my pen, smile, walk over.

—Afternoon.

—Afternoon.

We kiss, hold hands. He has a plastic bag.

—Lovely, this.

—Isn't it? So peaceful.

—That view is amazing.

I look, proud as if it were mine. The silence comes again, and I like it.

—Would you like tea? I just brewed a pot.

—Love it. I'm gasping.

I lead him by the hand. Where the tables are, there's a slight overlook, and you can see everything. Seth's head swivels, doesn't stop.

—Fantastic. Smell that air!

—You should stay sometime. It works wonders, believe me.

—I can see that, he says, and I smile. I pour tea.

—Milk, sugar?

—Just milk, thanks. I'm trying to cut the sugar out.

—Good call, I say, passing the cup. It is small, dainty, dwarfed between Seth's fingers.

—How did you find this?

—Ida, I say. The owners are friends with her son, he owns a place nearby.

—I see, he says, sipping. I'm glad that's sorted. You and her.

—Yes, well, I say, and look downhill, at the sheep. A bird shoots past, toward the house, where it disappears.

—Cor, bloody hell, Seth says.

—A swallow. They nest in the eaves. Must be feeding her young.

—Look at you, Bev Attenborough.

—*You* are so not funny.

—You are, he says, and I give his fingers a light slap, more a touch really.

—So I take it you're enjoying yourself? The flat's nice?

—Yes, a granny, but nice. I spend most of the time out here, for obvious reasons. I spread my arms wide. He's watching. It's perfect.

—So why are you leaving?

My arms fall. My smile too. I reach for my teacup.

—Can't stay forever. Cooped in a granny flat for months on end.

—You could go back.

—No, I couldn't, I say, in a tone I hope is final. I squint. Anyway, I've booked the tickets. Nonrefundable.

Seth sets down his cup, shows me his back. I stand and put my hands on his shoulders. Kiss his neck.

—Seth. Come on now.

—I'm okay.

—You'll start me off.

—I'm okay. Really.

I knead his shoulders, caught in the rough pleasure of feeling individual muscles beneath his clothes, imagine for a moment, chase thoughts away. Not right, not here.

—We'll come back, I say.

—I've got family in Black Rock. My brother went home years ago. I'll give you the address. He'll look after you.

—That would be wonderful.

He leans his head against me and the weight almost pushes me off balance. I brace myself. I like the pressure. There's a scrunch of gravel, slow, in steady time, and we look up, toward the house.

—Hey, Seth says.

—Afternoon, I say.

—Hey, how's it goin? Wills smiles.

He's on crutches, swinging toward us, but I'm still amazed at the change. His eyes are alert, and he's put on weight. He smiles at everyone, all the time. He works around the table, hops behind the chair Seth has pulled, falls into the seat, and smiles again, apologetically. There are scones in white paper bags, containers with jam and butter. He reaches.

—The man's got his priorities right, Seth says.

—Anyone want one?

—No thanks, I smile.

—Of course, Seth says, and they laugh.

He butters and spreads the scones, and we take in the breeze, the chatter of birds. Wills stretches his leg. The cast is thick, going from his chest and down his left leg. It's starting to blacken like rain clouds. We can't go anywhere until it comes off, three weeks from now. I am itchy to leave, impatient.

—Oh! Seth says, mouth full, wiping crumbs. I almost forgot.

He opens his plastic bag, digs, places a box on the table. A woman on the side, kissing a baby who looks into the camera. In large white type the box says, DNA TEST, and in smaller writing underneath, *For Paternity*. The box is blue.

—How much?

—Don't you worry how much, he says.

—Why paternity?

Seth shrugs.

—Well, for most cases the fatherhood's in dispute. Just put down your names with some identification and leave the father blank, it should be fine. That's what they said.

—And then?

—You send it off. It's £129 for the lab test, plus postage. They deliver anywhere in the UK.

I whistle beneath my breath. Wills picks up the box.

—It's tiny, he says.

—Just swabs and packaging, Seth replies.

I tell myself I'll bear that in mind.

❦

Wills goes for a walk to the bottom of the hill, leaves us. He's very astute. I watch him pick his way across grass, trying to avoid holes and mud patches. He stops, peers at the sky.

—Nice lad, Seth says.

I squeeze my smile against teeth.

—What?

Taking his hand, ducking my head.

—I want to give you something, I say. For all you've done. And to apologize.

I bend over the table, write something for him, something personal, sign my name and close the journal. I hand it to him.

—There you are.

He's gaping again.

—Don't you need it?

—I have a copy. On my computer. You can have this.

He runs his fingers along the cover, turns it. I shiver.

—What for?

—To explain, I say, and feel my eyes tear.

—I don't mean to sound ungrateful.

—You don't. I was. And now I'm not.

I get to my feet, thinking of his warmth, of being close, and Tamar begins to bark from somewhere inside the house. I squint into sunlight, which is directly in my eyes, and the trees around me sway, and there's a flash of shadow and light, stuttering strobe. I try to find Wills, see him moving steadily toward the pond, prompting a scattering of sheep. Tamar's sharp barks are louder. My eyes sting, overflow. I find it difficult to breathe. I hear movement, feel Seth call my name, and Wills is swinging closer toward the pond, and the trees are rustling soft, disgruntled mutters, and something wells up inside me. I'm holding my hand to my throat, trying to call him. I want to tell him to watch out, but I can't find my voice and he's too far away. The intensity is so strong it almost floors me. I reach out, and the rustle of the trees grows stronger, and I remember this, not a concept or a disembodied word, but an actual emotion, love from my crown to the balls of my feet. There's a pinprick tickle of sensation in my fingers. I try harder to exhale but I can't. There are lights, colors, and I can feel an ache in my cheeks, before I realize I'm smiling. I'm smiling and trying to ignore that hollow feeling, the ache of the faux silence of my flat, the chorus of raw, harsh breath. It strikes me still, half-grinning into the breeze. Wills swings away from the pond, across the shorn field, and the air leaves my body in one long burst.

Seth is behind me, big strong arms around my shoulders. Crooning, stroking my head. He cradles me against him, and the roughness of his sweater scrapes my cheeks. I don't mind, this is good pain, the best I've felt in ages. I hold him, and hug him, and don't let go.

Also available from Akashic Books

GATHERING OF WATERS
a novel by Bernice L. McFadden
250 pages, trade paperback original, $15.95

"McFadden works a kind of miracle—not only do [her characters] retain their appealing humanity; their story eclipses the bonds of history to offer continuous surprises . . . Beautiful and evocative, *Gathering of Waters* brings three generations to life . . . The real power of the narrative lies in the richness and complexity of the characters. While they inhabit these pages they live, and they do so gloriously and messily and magically, so that we are at last sorry to see them go, and we sit with those small moments we had with them and worry over them, enchanted, until they become something like our own memories, dimmed by time, but alive with the ghosts of the past, and burning with spirits." —Jesmyn Ward, *New York Times Book Review*

SONG FOR NIGHT
a novella by Chris Abani
164 pages, trade paperback original, $12.95

"Chris Abani might be the most courageous writer working right now. There is no subject matter he finds daunting, no challenge he fears. Aside from that, he's stunningly prolific and writes like an angel. If you want to get at the molten heart of contemporary fiction, Abani is the starting point." —Dave Eggers, author of *What Is the What*

"*Song for Night* has the feel of a prose poem, with its primary focus on imagery and its spare, musical language. The lyrical intensity of the writing perfectly suits the material." —*Los Angeles Times*

"Abani works with a moral imperative to unravel the bizarre and corrupt practices that supposedly transform boys into men." —*Washington Post*

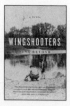

WINGSHOOTERS
a novel by Nina Revoyr
250 pages, trade paperback original, $15.95

"Revoyr does a remarkable job of conveying [protagonist] Michelle's lost innocence and fear through this accomplished story of family and the dangers of complacency in the face of questionable justice." —*Publishers Weekly*, starred review

"Revoyr writes rhapsodically of a young girl's enthrallment to the natural world and charts, with rising intensity, her resilient narrator's painful awakening to human failings and senseless violence. In this shattering northern variation on *To Kill a Mockingbird*, Revoyr drives to the very heart of tragic ignorance, unreason, and savagery." —*Booklist*, starred review

A MIND OF WINTER
a novel by Shira Nayman
320 pages, trade paperback original, $15.95

"Nayman's saga delves deeply into how even those not directly affected are forever changed by war." —*Publishers Weekly*

"With insight and a dazzling imagination, Shira Nayman transports us into a web of post–World War II lives, from Shanghai, to London, to Long Island. As in her previous works, Nayman's characters show us the long shadow that war casts on memory, identity, and love."
—Nancy Sherman, author of *The Untold War*

GOD CARLOS
a novel by Anthony C. Winkler
196 pages, trade paperback original, $15.95

"Readers are transported along to Jamaica, in Winkler's richly invented 16th century, where his flawless prose paints their slice of time, in turn both brutally graphic and lyrically gorgeous. This is a thoroughly engaging adventure story from renowned Jamaican author Winkler, sure to enchant readers who treasure a fabulous tale exquisitely rendered." —*Library Journal*

"A tale of the frequently tragic—and also comic—clash of races and religions brought on by colonization . . . Anthony Winkler spins an enlightening parable, rich in historical detail and irony."
—*Shelf Awareness*

KINGSTON NOIR
edited by Colin Channer
288 pages, trade paperback original, $15.95

Brand-new stories by: Marlon James, Kwame Dawes, Patricia Powell, Chris Abani, Colin Channer, Marcia Douglas, Leone Ross, Kei Miller, Christopher John Farley, Ian Thomson, and Thomas Glave.

From Trench Town to Half Way Tree to Norbrook to Portmore and beyond, the stories of *Kingston Noir* shine light into the darkest corners of this fabled city. Together, these outstanding tales comprise the best volume of short fiction ever to arise from the literary wellspring that is Jamaica.